SHADOWS 8

SHADOWS 8

EDITED BY CHARLES L. GRANT

DOUBLEDAY & COMPANY, INC.
GARDEN CITY, NEW YORK
1985

ISBN: 0-385-19823-X
Copyright © 1985 by Charles L. Grant
All rights reserved
Printed in the United States of America
First Edition

CONTENTS

6 *Contents*

INTRODUCTION

BY CHARLES L. GRANT

Part of the fun of scaring yourself either at a movie or by reading is that you know you can pull back from that fear, or that apprehension, whenever you want to. It's a safety valve of sorts, to keep you from thinking about what's really going on—about the killing, the possibility of a real supernatural world, the reflection of yourself you may see, or refuse to see, in the character(s) you're dealing with.

This withdrawal takes several forms: you turn away, you close the book, you nudge your neighbor, you laugh when it's over to prove you weren't scared a bit. You weren't, of course, even the slightest bit nervous. What you saw, on the screen or in your mind's own private theater, was nothing more than a shadow-play. Like someone casting a light on the wall and using his hands to create elephants and dogs and butterflies and geese.

There are, however, other shadows.

They do not reflect the kindnesses of the world, or the cute and cuddly things one finds under a Christmas tree, or the laughter that casts away all demons.

There are shadows which are much too grim even to smile at, because they look, even in silhouette, too much like the dreams we have that we do not admit to, like the people we fear are living within us contained only by the fact that we are, after all, a civilized people.

These are the shadows that make us squirm, close the book, look away, and make us feel all too alone with what we cannot share with our neighbor, with what we cannot cast away by a simple false laugh.

Sometimes shadows are no fun at all.

Charles L. Grant
Newton, New Jersey
December 1984

EDITOR'S NOTE

Since the beginning of this series, seven volumes ago, I have included notes at the beginning of each story which have, in some fashion, expanded on whatever I was talking about in the Introduction. There are no notes this time. Pat LoBrutto (Doubleday's editor) and I have agreed that this time, considering the stories' somewhat grim contents, we'll forgo my intrusions on the authors' work.

C.L.G.

SHADOWS 8

EVERYTHING'S GOING TO BE ALL RIGHT

by Gene DeWeese

At dusk on the third day after her unremembered death, Amelia Wilson drifted slowly into wakefulness. Beyond the curtained bedroom window, outlined against the fading redness of the western sky, she could see the autumn skeleton of the oak her grandparents had planted long before her birth.

But why, she wondered dully, was she still in bed so late in the day?

Things were not as they normally were, she realized, and that thought troubled her. Something must have happened to upset her daily routine, but she couldn't remember what it could have been, and that troubled her even more.

For a long time she lay perfectly still, trying to feel the weight and texture of the blanket across her body, trying to feel the warmth it had always given her. Her eyes moved slowly about the shadowy room, taking in the familiar, comforting shapes—the bureau, the mirrored dressing table, the tiny nightstand within easy reach of her side of the bed. All were the same as they had always been, and that, she knew, was good. The door to the closet, the huge, walk-in closet her father had built the year before he had died, stood half open, but that was not unusual. The door to the hall—

She felt a puzzled frown drawing at her features as she saw that the door to the hall was tightly closed. Except when there were guests—John's sister or one of his brothers, more often than not—the bedroom door was never closed. With no one but herself and John in the house, there was no need. When she had been growing up, when this had been her parents' room, the door had often been closed.

Except, she thought with a sudden, snuggling warmth, for those winter nights when the wind had howled and frost had built its icy patterns on the windows and her parents had opened the door and invited her to share the bed with them. It hadn't happened often, but those nights, with all their warmth and security around her, had been the best that she could remember. But they had come to an end—

They *had* come to an end, she told herself grimly, and now it was John that gave her the warmth and security, not just on those rare, wintry nights but every night of every year.

But where, she wondered abruptly, *was* John? Why had he let her sleep the day away like this? He *always* awakened her before he left for the office in the morning, and certainly, even if he had forgotten just this once or she had gone back to sleep after he left, he would have awakened her when he returned home and found her, incredibly, still in bed.

Surely, she thought, he must be home by now. It was autumn, but until daylight saving time ended, in another few weeks, he was always home well before dark. And if for any reason he was going to be late, he called her. Always.

Where *was* he? Had something happened to him?

With an effort, she raised herself to her feet and wondered why her limbs were so sluggish, why her head seemed caught in a whirl of dizziness.

I've slept too long, she told herself. *That's all. My mind isn't working very well, and apparently my body isn't either. But it'll be all right. As soon as I move around a little and get my thoughts organized, everything will be all right.*

Downstairs in the kitchen, she stood looking around, absorbing the familiarity of the place. The same table—sturdy hardwood, not unsightly plastic—that she had eaten at as a child stood beneath the shadowy windows that looked out into the side yard with its elm and walnut trees beyond the narrow drive. The bulletin board next to the refrigerator, oddly empty now, had once held not only notes and reminders and recipes but, for brief periods every few weeks, the report cards she had proudly carried home.

It was a comforting feeling, just standing there, but a trace of a shiver ran through her as she remembered those later times, when she and John had gone on trips and spent each night in a new and different room in a new and different town. She had enjoyed the sights during the days, particularly the autumn hills of Maine and Vermont, but she would have enjoyed them all the more if, at the end of each day, she had been able to return here, to these familiar surroundings.

With a smile, she remembered how John had laughed when she told him how she felt. "Maybe next year we can rent an R.V.," he had said. "Those things are practically houses on wheels."

And one year, she remembered, they had done just that. It had been better, but it still hadn't been the same as coming home each evening would have been. But they had enjoyed themselves, and when they had come back—

Abruptly, the sluggish memories fell away as she heard a car turning into the drive. A moment later, the glow of headlights seemed to fill the darkened kitchen. Hurrying to the window, she looked out as the lights were doused.

It wasn't, she realized with a new twinge of uneasiness, John's car, but it had stopped in front of the closed garage doors. And John was climbing out of the passenger's side. A woman in a dark dress and hat had been driving, and she was getting out too and walking around the car and taking John's arm.

Only as the two made their way up the steps to the kitchen door and John flipped on the outside light before fitting his key into the lock did Amelia realize that the woman was John's sister, Ellen. It was, she realized with a renewed touch of uneasiness, the first time in years she had seen Ellen wearing anything but jeans and a sweater. It had been at their father's funeral, she remembered, just after Ellen had graduated from Walker State. Even then, at the graduation, under her black robes, she had been wearing her "everyday" clothes.

And John—for the first time, Amelia realized that John was wearing a suit, his only suit. His wedding and funeral suit, he called it, since those were the only times she had ever seen him wear it. Before she met him, he had worn it to apply for his job at Barker Engineering in Granger, but by the time they had started going together, he had slipped back to sport jackets and open-collared shirts.

But there had been one other time, she thought with a frown. Just recently, just a few days ago, he had gotten it out of the closet and put it on. He had gone somewhere, and when he had come back—

Sharply, she pushed the memory away before it could become clear, before her suddenly growing uneasiness could escalate into open fear.

Whatever the memory was, she didn't want it back, not now. John was here, he was opening the back door this very second, and there was no need for her to remember, no need at all.

Then the door was open and he was striding in, peeling off the jacket as he walked, pulling the tie loose and unbuttoning the collar. Dropping the jacket on the back of a chair, he jerked open the refrigerator door and wrenched an ice-cube tray from the freezer.

"Want one?" he asked, glancing at his sister as he took a bottle from the cabinet over the sink.

Ellen shook her head. "I have to drive home yet."

Taking down a large tumbler, he dropped in a pair of ice cubes and began to pour the amber liquid.

"You better take it a little easy yourself," Ellen said quietly. Her hat was off, and she was standing, leaning her back against the door. "You know what your head is like the morning after."

"It couldn't be any worse than it is right now!" he snapped, half draining the glass in a single gulp, grimacing at the taste.

"Damn it, Johnnie!" Ellen flared. "We've all told you a dozen times already, but I'll tell you once more anyway! You can't blame yourself! *She's* the one who took the damn pills! All you did was get yourself a decent job, for God's sake!"

"Sure, three hundred miles away! And then I tell her if she won't come with me, I'm going anyway! Just like that!" He snorted in self-directed anger. "Mr. Tact! That's me all the way!"

"So what were you supposed to do? Stick it out with Barker all your life, just because Amelia refused to move out of this seven-room womb? Damn it, Johnnie, that just doesn't make sense!"

"I know, I know! But that doesn't make it any easier!" He gulped down the rest of the drink and dropped onto one of the chairs at the table, his hands completely enveloping the empty glass.

"Neither will that, not in the long run," Ellen said, fingering the bottle where he had set it on the table earlier.

"Maybe not, but right now I'm just working on the short run. All right?"

Ellen lowered herself onto the chair across the corner of the table from him. Gently, she closed her hands around his. "You want to stay with Al and me? I guess we can put up with you for the three or four days until you get things wrapped up here and make the move."

He shook his head. "Hell, *I* can't put up with me right now. No, I'll be okay till then. But if you want to help sort through her clothes and things some weekend, I wouldn't object."

Ellen nodded, blinking back a tear, and for a long time there was only silence while Amelia stood by, watching and yet not watching. She had stopped listening, *really* listening, almost the moment they had come in. They had acted as if she were not even there, and it had hurt, just as that sort of thing had always hurt. But this time there had been a special pain, a sharp, bitter ache that seemed to close around her and seep through her like a poisonous mist, and she had stopped listening. She had willed away the sound and with it the pain until, finally, both had begun to fade.

And then they were alone. Ellen had gone, Amelia couldn't remember when. John lay sprawled on the couch, the flickering TV set the only light in the room. The news was on, she noticed, and she wondered how much time had passed without her noticing. It seemed like only minutes ago that he and Ellen had come into the kitchen and the pain had begun and—

"Damn you, Amelia!" John's voice was little more than a whisper, but it cut through the haze of sound from the TV set like a knife. "Damn you, damn you, *damn* you!"

And then he was on his feet, moving unsteadily through the flickering darkness to the stairway, and Amelia, unable this time to hold back the pain, was following.

And as she followed, as the pain washed over her, she was equally unable to keep the memories away, the despairing memories of his harsh, unbending words, his unbreakable determination, and her own inability to accept or understand.

And her fear. She remembered the churning heaviness in her stomach. She remembered the numbness at the thought of leaving this place, the only home she had ever known, and she remembered the actual physical pain when she finally realized, beyond a doubt, that nothing she could ever say would stop him.

But it was not too late. It couldn't be too late, even now. They had had arguments before, disagreements, and they had always been able to work them out, somehow.

And then the pain was gone, submerged in a new sense of hope that was welling up within her.

Slowly, beginning to smile, she went to the guest bedroom where she knew he now lay. He had gone there that first night, but that time she had not followed him, the way she had all the other times over the years. But now she would.

As she moved, other memories filtered to the surface of her thoughts, memories of other disagreements, other nights in this room. They had called it their "making up room." In the middle of the night, she would leave their regular bedroom, at the other end of the hall, and come to where he lay. And always, in the middle of the night, after each of them had had time to rest and sleep on whatever the quarrel had been about, they would make up.

She smiled again, remembering. Somehow, those nights were better, more tender than other nights. It was as if, on those nights alone, they would truly know each other.

And that is how it would be tonight, now that she remembered, now that she knew what had to be done.

Later—perhaps minutes, perhaps hours—she found herself at the door once again, sliding silently through it, feeling her negligee brush lightly against the doorframe.

As always, he lay on his back, arms and legs sprawled in all directions. In the dim light from the street lamp outside, she could see his chest rise and fall with each breath, and in the silence she could hear the faintest trace of a snore.

She sat on the edge of the bed, placing herself between him and the curtained window, and the familiar ritual began. Softly, she reached out and touched his forehead with her hand, then brushed her fingers lightly over his cheek. As her hand touched his chin, felt the rasp of eighteen hours' growth of beard, he stirred. One hand slid from beneath the sheet and brushed at hers. An almost inaudible moan came from his lips.

"It's all right, honey," she whispered and leaned forward. "I was wrong. I'll go with you wherever you want to go. Everything's going to be all right."

And it would be. She knew. In the morning, when they awakened together, everything would again be all right.

She pulled her legs up onto the bed and lay down across his outstretched arm. Soon, she knew, he would awaken to her touch, and the arm would curl around her, drawing her close.

Waiting, she laid her head on the pillow and ran her hand lightly over his throat, then his chest. Again he stirred and rolled his head from side to side. When his face turned toward her, she kissed him, softly and lingeringly.

Pulling back, she could see a sleepy smile spreading across his face, and she could feel his arm moving beneath her. His eyes opened, just a slit, still clouded with sleep.

"Amelia?" His voice was fuzzy and slurred.

"I'm here. It's all right now. I'm here, and I always will be." She snuggled against him, forcing her arms around him.

"Amelia? Is that you?" His body moved slowly, sleepily, responding to her touch, her voice. She shifted her weight, bringing her parted lips to his neck, then to his shoulder as the collar of his pajamas fell open.

Then, in an instant, his eyes snapped open and his whole body stiffened. For a second, his eyes were blank, but suddenly they focused. She could feel his heart begin to pound.

"It's all right, honey. I'm here now," she whispered softly, but he sat up abruptly, almost knocking her from the bed.

"Amelia?" His eyes darted about the darkened room as if she didn't exist. His hand brushed past her and touched the spots on his neck that she had kissed.

For a moment, a chill flowed over her and a memory of the pain stabbed at her mercilessly. The ritual was being broken, and she didn't know why. She was giving in to him, even in this, and still he was not responding. But there was nothing more she could do. She could only wait and hope.

Finally, he lowered his fingers from the spot on his neck. He frowned as he glanced at the fingers, then looked around the room once more. There was a deep breath then, drawn unevenly, and a ragged sigh. Slowly, with a collapsing motion, he lay down. His eyes blinked several times, and moisture glistened on his cheeks. Then, as if with a special effort, he closed his eyes.

For a long time, she watched, letting the memory of the pain and the broken ritual fade. Then, beginning to smile again, she leaned forward, reaching out to touch him once more. Everything was going to be all right. They had always been able to work things out somehow. They always had and they always would, as long as they were together.

CYCLES

by Kim Antieau

They have a name for what is wrong with me, I am told. I say there isn't anything wrong with me that I'm not taking care of myself. Young people, especially women, often have this problem, my mother tells me. Later my grandmother tells me again.

It doesn't matter what they say to me; I won't eat. Or if I do, I go into the bathroom, lock the door and stick my finger down my throat. They don't realize I have to stop the thing from growing inside of me.

Six days a week, I work at the restaurant across the street from the restaurant where my mother works. It is not the fanciest part of town, nor is it the worst. It is only a twenty-minute walk from our apartment, and the whores, drunks, and junkies are at a minimum. My mother tells me I should be grateful we have jobs. My grandmother reminds me that her mother worked herself to death as a washerwoman. Often, my mother and grandmother seem to be the same person when they speak, only one is twenty years older than the other.

Once, I wandered into the university area and heard two women talking about their jobs. They were attractive college types, with wavy brown hair and cashmere sweaters.

"I like waitressing at the Pub," one of them said. "I meet so many interesting people!"

She seemed to bubble when she talked. I moved into the shade of an oak tree to listen unobserved. They were like two bright flowers in the sun.

"Yeah, I hear the theater people and some profs hang out there."

Someone came up to them then, and they walked away. Some days later I went by the Pub and stood outside. Inside, it was crowded and noisy and filled with well-dressed, laughing people. I saw pretty young things stuffing dollar bills into their pretty little aprons. It was no wonder the campus flower enjoyed her work. I get nickeled and dimed all day.

At home, it is all too obvious I don't eat. Grandma bends over her needlepoint (she sells it to a gift store downtown; they pay her minimum prices and then jack the retail price up five times or more) and urges me to have some dinner. She squints too much and coughs. When she turned thirty-five, she gave up smoking, but she still has the cough. She went to the doctor for it once and was told she needed to get out of the city. "Move?" she had asked. When the doctor said, "Yes, that would be best," she had laughed herself into another coughing fit. My mother quit smoking when she was thirty-five too. I never started. I suppose that is one way in which I differ from my mother.

It is not like I don't want to eat. I do. But I believe I am the only one who can stop this cycle, so I must do what I must do. I think about food all of the time. Every moment of the day I think about all the ways not to eat. Each morsel I reject is another victory for me: I am surrounded by eating people all day and still I don't take a bite. It gives me courage and strength. Perhaps I can conquer after all.

I realized early on that if I didn't eat at all, I'd die. And that is certainly not the point. The thing in me can die. Not me. So I eat a little bit when I deem it necessary. If I feel my body pulling at my muscles, eating them for energy, I go into the kitchen when everyone is asleep and nibble on something. Once, Grandma came in and I hid the food behind my back.

"Child, it is not a sin to eat," she said. "You pay for it. Eat it."

She does not understand. They both get angry with me.

"Just eat!" my mother said one day. I could tell she wanted to take a handful of food and cram it down my throat. "Just force yourself to eat!"

I stared at her. She started to cry.

"I suppose it is all my fault?" she said, sinking into the kitchen chair. It wobbled as she sat down. They are old, and we need new ones. "I've been reading about it. They say maybe you don't want to grow up. It seems kind of silly, since you're already eighteen years old. I just don't understand."

She left the room, and Grandma took her place, crying and shaking her head. Was it she who I would look like in forty years?

I think about what my mother said, about not wanting to grow up. It is one of the stupidest things I've ever heard. Who doesn't want to grow up unless it is some woman nearly forty years old like my mother who looks back at her life and realizes it was a waste? I want to grow up, to get away.

Sometimes I go out with Billy, one of our neighbors, but he becomes concerned about me, and he is too tired and old for his age. He talks about his sister and her husband who beats her, about his father and mother who drink too much. After a time I tire of him, too, and instead I spend my free time not eating or looking through the family album. Mostly the album is filled with pictures of Grandma, Mother, and myself. There are various relatives, but I don't know them anymore. A tall, handsome man with a beret is supposed to be my grandfather, but I don't believe it.

I grow weak at work. My boss tells me I should take some time off. He doesn't want to fire me, but he will soon, I know. It will kill me after all, won't it, if I lose my job?

I go to the library and study science magazines. I try to verify what I have suspected for some time. My grandmother had my mother when she was eighteen. My mother had me when she was eighteen. All three of us were born almost on the same date. I look at the photographs in the album and we are all the same, just different ages, living out the same life again and again. Sometimes I awaken at night, terrified, and it takes me a few seconds to realize this night terror is not mine but one my mother had when she was my age, or my grandmother.

My mother threatens to put me in a hospital, but we have no insurance, and she would never put me in a state hospital. She and Grandma take me to the neighborhood clinic. Because of my income, they say, I won't have to pay much. The doctor is rough and rude. He thinks he's God in his white uniform. He wants to know who I've been sleeping with. I stare at the wall and don't answer him. It is none of his business, but I haven't had sex with anyone in a long time. He would not, of course, believe in the virgin birth or spontaneous parthenogenesis, as the magazine article called it.

He shakes his head and says, "You people. Don't you know what contraceptives are? How are you going to pay for an abortion, or a baby, for that matter?"

I want to rip out his eyes, slice off his testicles, something that would be long drawn out and painful. What could he possibly know of my life, when he lives in the Heights and visits here once a week or once a month so he can feel superior?

Instead, I leave. It is too late. I have tried not feeding it. It didn't work. I don't think I understood, really, until now. Abortion is not even an option.

They ask me to leave my job. I am showing too much. My boss puts his arm across my shoulders as I cry. He promises I can have my job back afterward. Grandma and Mother tell me which agencies to go to for help. They have been through it before. I start smoking, just as Grandma and Mother did when they were pregnant. I know it is not good for either of us, but I can't seem to help myself. At night I dream nightmares that are not my own. She is screaming already for me to let her out of her misery. I cannot, I cannot. I eat and sleep, and Mom and Grandma tell the neighbors I am better. I suppose it is more honorable to have a pregnant daughter than one who doesn't eat.

When I go into labor—I am early, just as my mother and grand-mother were—I hear cries and feel pain that seem to be from someone other than myself, but someone who is myself. I wonder if either my grandmother or mother realized the truth. The baby comes out quietly. She is female, as I knew she would be, with a crown of black hair.

Suddenly she begins to cry. I cry too. Her tiny lungs pause for air and then she begins screaming in earnest. I open my mouth, and the sound I emit is identical to hers. The hospital staff in the room halt their routines and look at us. The screaming frightens the nurse, and she practically drops the baby on my stomach. I hold her tightly against me. I know the pain she feels. I have felt it for generations. Now she will feel it again. I hold her close and I am holding myself, my mother, my grandmother. The cycle will not end.

Someone else is crying now, someone who is not a part of us. I rock my baby against me, saying, "There, there." Her crying has stopped, and she lies quietly against my chest.

The doctor puts his fingers against my baby's neck.

"These people," he says, shaking his head, reminding me of the other doctor. He motions to the nurse, and she takes the baby from me. I feel tired and relieved. Perhaps it will be all right. Perhaps I am wrong, and the chain can be broken. "Life means so little to them," the doctor continues. "They don't know how to use contraceptives, constantly having children. Jesus." He slams his fist against the door and leaves the room. I hear the nurse sobbing; someone else is saying something about a broken neck.

My eyes widen and I call to them, asking for my baby, but she is gone. They all look over at me.

"Should we call the police or was it an accident?"

"Just let her alone," one says. "Can't you see she's half crazy and half starved? She probably didn't realize her own strength. The baby is dead. Let's just let the episode drop."

Dead? I bolt up and clutch my stomach.

"It's all right," one of the nurses says, touching my arm. "You're all right. It's over now."

Months later, I sit in our apartment in the wobbly chair, smoking and listening to Grandmother and Mother talk. I remember what the nurse said about it being all over, and I know now it will never end. I *am* different from my mother and grandmother. I touch my abdomen. Inside, I have begun all over again.

THE TUCKAHOE

by Nancy Etchemendy

It's getting on toward dark, and I keep hoping maybe I've caught a fever and I'm out of my head. Maybe there isn't anything waiting under the house to get me as soon as I step outside. Maybe Pa and Lemmy are just playing a trick on me, and they'll come strutting through the front door any minute now, smug as a couple of tom turkeys. Oh, how I'd like that. Pa, he'd laugh at me, because that's his way, to make a joke out of Ruben, who'll never be a man. And Lemmy would probably hook his thumbs in his belt and call me his sissy little brother, seeing me wrapped up in Momma's quilt like this, shaking, and nothing sticking out except my nose and the barrel of Grampa's Colt pistol. But I wouldn't mind. It would be all right, just this once. If they come in here alive and whole, if they could prove tuckahoe is just tuckahoe, and that empty thing on the porch isn't really what's left of Momma. Then they could laugh all they want, and it would be all right. Just this once.

The rain started in again a couple hours ago, just like last night. Makes my heart crawl up into my throat and lie there twitching like a half-dead frog. I lit all the lamps and tried to make a fire in the fireplace. But the fire, it don't seem to burn right. It looks just the way I feel, puny and wavery, like it might not be here in the morning. I tried to give myself a good talking-to, just like Momma would if she saw me now. "Ruben," she'd say, "the Lord helps them that helps themselves." But I don't think the Lord had much to do with this rain, nor with the thing that ate Momma.

Last night, when the storm first started, I had a feeling this wasn't any regular rain. Didn't seem natural the way it poured out of the sky. It came down in long, wavy curtains, like somebody'd emptied a bunch of big tin washtubs all at one time. There weren't any drops at all except from the splashes when it hit the ground. And the lightning felt wrong too. I've never seen such lightning before. Why, it lit up the sky blue and white all night long, one bolt right after another. Early on in the evening, it hit the two big poplars down by the road, both at the same time. Before the rain put the fire out, they were burnt to pure cinders, and there was nothing left this morning except black poles.

The thing that made my skin creep worst of all, though, was the smell. I usually like the smell of rain, especially this time of year, when the tree sap is running and the ground is already a little damp. But this smelled funny, kind of like that oily stuff Pa sprays on the crops sometimes to kill the bugs. I told Pa that. I said the rain smelled real bad, like oil or something. I even went out on the porch and got a little on my fingers so he could smell it for himself.

But Pa, he has a stubborn streak, and most of the time he doesn't pay attention till something turns around and bites him right on the toe. He looked at me kind of sideways, scratching his beard, and he said, "Ruben, I don't smell a blame thing. Quit acting like an old woman." And Lemmy made it worse by laughing outright.

I saw right then I might as well not waste any more breath on those two, so I just shut my mouth and went over to the table to watch Momma kneading bread. I like to watch her when she has her sleeves rolled up and her hands all covered with flour. Sometimes a lock of fine, brown hair falls down in her eyes, and she asks me if I'll tuck it back for her. Last night, when I tucked her hair back in, she whispered, "The rain don't smell right to me, neither, if you want to know the truth." Remembering that now makes me feel like crying.

After a while, I lay down by the fire and tried to read in one of my schoolbooks about this fellow who'd discovered the South Pole, but it wasn't any use. I kept getting this stickery feeling all up and down my back. Made me think Lemmy or somebody had sneaked up behind me and was trying to scare me. But every time I twisted around to look, there was nobody there at all, just the front window lit up all cold and blue, and the curtains of rain outside, and the roar of thunder. The more I stared at that book, the more I thought about the window, and the queerer I felt about what I might see through it if I turned around again. The hairs on my arms and the back of my neck stood up, and pretty soon a cold sweat broke out on my lip, right where I'm starting to get a few little mustache hairs. I made up my mind the only way to get myself over being afraid was to go take a good long look through the window to prove there was nothing peering in, fearsome or otherwise.

I put my book down on the rug where I'd been lying, and I got up and walked to the window, which was misted over a little on account of its being warmer inside than out. I spit on my sleeve and rubbed a little place in the glass. I couldn't see really good, because the rain and lightning made everything look so different. The straw grass on the front acre might have been a stranger's pond, and Momma's chicken coop loomed up in the night like one of those dinosaurs I've seen in books. I squinted for a long time, and finally after I had things figured out a little, I saw the chickens were all riled up, flapping around in the rain. That struck me as just plain unnatural, for chickens are pretty much like people when it comes to staying indoors on a wet night.

Then I saw the other thing, and it gave me a chill so deep I felt like I'd been dropped down a well. Through that little place in the glass, I made out something creeping towards the root cellar. I stood still as a lump of salt to get a better look, though my blood was hammering inside my veins, and my knees felt like cheese. The next bolt of lightning lit up everything almost as clear as day, and just for a second, even with the rain, I got a perfect sight of the thing.

There's a funny kind of toadstool that grows down in the dimmest part of the woods. Tuckahoe, Pa calls them, but Momma says they aren't like any tuckahoe she's ever seen, and we aren't to eat them under any circumstances. I wouldn't want to anyway, for the sight of them makes my stomach turn somersaults. You never find just one or two, coming up separately around dead wood like regular mushrooms. These tuckahoe like to grow from the heart of a living tree, a hundred or more together in a slippery, gray clump, like overgrown frogs' eggs. No single one of them is bigger than a man's thumb, but I've seen nests two feet around stuck onto unlucky maples and dogwoods. Lemmy, he gets bored sometimes and knocks the clumps down and hacks them up with a stick for fun. But me, I'd rather stay as far away from them as I can.

Tuckahoe. That's what I thought of as I watched that thing crawl across our front acre in the stinking rain. I felt the sweat gathering into little streams on my forehead while I told myself to stop and think. It couldn't be tuckahoe, because it was too big, big as a man. Besides that, it was moving, and darn fast, too. Tuckahoe couldn't move by itself, not that I ever heard of anyway.

I could feel a howl building up in my throat, getting ready to come out whether I wanted it to or not, when all of a sudden there was a big crash from the back of the house and the whole place shook. I think I did let out a yell then, but nobody paid any attention, because they were all running to see what had caused the commotion. By the time I got my wits together enough to follow them, Pa and Lemmy were standing by the back door looking out into the storm. A good-sized limb from the old oak tree by the kitchen had broken loose in the wind and come down on the roof. Pa was growling and cursing, and Momma was out in the rain with a *Farm Journal* over her head, trying to see if the roof was all right.

All I could think of was that thing crawling around out there, and I said, "Get her back inside! Get her out of the rain!" My voice cracked, just like it always does when I most wish it wouldn't.

And Lemmy gave me one of those cockeyed half smiles of his and said, "For Pete's sake. You'd think she's made of sugar or something. The rain won't melt her, you know."

Then I hit Lemmy in the stomach, and he hit me in the nose. And the next thing I knew, Momma was standing over me with an ice pack, yelling a blue streak, and dripping rainwater all over the kitchen floor. I didn't care. I just closed my eyes and let her yell. As long as she was back inside, that's all that mattered to me.

I remember lying in bed this morning thinking the tuckahoe thing must have been nothing but a bad dream. I heard birds chirping outside the window, and I watched a little finger of sunlight move across a spiderweb in the corner. The rain had stopped, and the clouds were no more than a few raggedy strings way up high. I felt so good that I whistled while I put my pants on, and said good morning to Lemmy even though my nose was still pretty sore.

Momma was getting ready to go out and fetch the eggs from the chickens, like she does every morning. She had to pull on a pair of high rubber boots, because the front acre was ankle-deep in mud from the storm. I stood in the sunshine on the porch and watched her wade out towards the chicken coop. She had a basket hanging from one arm for the eggs. She got about ten or fifteen steps away, then stopped dead still with the basket swinging from her elbow. She turned around, and the look on her face made me swallow without meaning to.

"There's something kind of funny out here, Ruben," she said. "Better ask Pa to come and take a look."

I hollered for Pa, and he grumbled, for he hates to get up from his chair. But he lumbered out into the mud, and Lemmy and I rolled up our pants and followed him.

Momma had come across a patch of slimy stuff. It could have been egg whites maybe, except it was sort of milky, and where would egg whites come from anyway, when there were no yolks or shells lying around? Pa frowned at it, and he and Lemmy stuck their fingers in it. Then Pa said it wasn't anything to worry about, probably some new kind of bug left it, or it might be some kind of mildew, he didn't know.

All that time, I was standing on one foot and then the other, and my heart was ticking fast as a two-dollar watch. I had a pretty fair idea what had left that slime, and it didn't have anything to do with bugs. "Pa," I said, "I think you should know I saw some kind of strange thing crawling around out here last night, looked like one of those tuckahoe clumps, only almost as big as you are."

Lemmy rolled his eyes and spit in the mud right by my foot. Pa just looked mad and said, "Ruben, everybody knows you can't tell the difference between a tall tale and the truth. If you think I'm gonna swallow a story like that, you've got a brain about the size of a pea." Then he and Lemmy sloshed back to the house, talking and laughing. I stayed outside with Momma, because I felt like I was either going to throw things or cry, and I didn't want to give Pa the satisfaction of seeing it.

By and by, Momma and I went and took a look at the chicken coop. It turned out there were hardly any eggs in the boxes. That was spooky enough. But what we found just inside the chicken wire scared me a lot worse. I thought I saw two rags lying there on the ground, but when I looked closer, I saw it wasn't rags at all. It was two dead hens, just their feathers and skin, with nothing inside. I squinted and poked, but I couldn't find any rips or bites. It was like all the blood and meat and bones had been sucked right out of them, leaving them empty, without a single mark.

Momma turned all white when she saw those hens, and she told Pa

about them as soon as we got back inside. But he treats her the same
way he treats me, like she hasn't got the sense she was born with. He
said to her, "What do you expect after a storm like that? If you were a
chicken would you lay a lot of eggs with all that racket goin' on?" Then
he said a coon must have gotten in and killed them.

I came pretty close to telling him right then and there that if he
expected me to swallow a story like that, he must have a brain about
the size of a pea. I know what a coon does to a chicken, and it doesn't
look anything like that. But I never really said it. I just thought it. And
now I'm glad, because all I want is just to see Pa alive, even if he's
wrong sometimes.

Momma took her boots off and went into the kitchen and lit the fire
in the gas range. She'd only gotten four eggs, and that was just two
apiece for Pa and Lemmy, even if Momma and I went without. Pa was
yelling about how he was half starved to death, and she couldn't very
well expect him to haul an oak limb down off the roof with a half-
empty stomach. He told her she'd better fry up a whole lot of spuds to
make up the difference, and he snapped his suspenders, which Momma
hates because it makes them wear out quicker.

Momma, she was busy with the griddle and slicing some bacon, and
she said to me without looking, "Ruben, honey, will you go down to
the root cellar and bring up some spuds?"

I just stood there. All of a sudden, it didn't matter how bright the
sun was shining or how loud the birds were twittering. It might as well
have been pitch dark and rain pouring down in buckets again as far as I
was concerned. I was thinking about that slime on the front acre and
those two empty chicken skins. And I could see the tuckahoe in my
head, all smeary through that window in the glare of the lightning,
headed straight for the root cellar.

Momma turned and frowned at me when I made no move for the
door. Then the frown melted off into worry lines, and she said,
"What's wrong, honey?"

"Momma, please don't make me go. There's something down
there," I said. My throat was so dry I could hardly get the words out.

Then Pa, he jumped up out of his chair and grabbed me by the shirt
and shook me. I saw the veins popping up on his big, thick neck, and
his face was the color of a ripe tomato. I'd have shut my eyes, but I
knew that would just make him madder, and I was scared that he'd

backhand me or kick me like he sometimes does. Instead, he opened up his mouth so those ragged, yellow teeth of his showed like an animal's against the furry dark of his beard. I could feel his breath tickling my cheeks, hot and sharp from the hard cider he'd already drunk that morning. I wished he liked me better. Oh, how I wished it.

"You're a good-for-nothin' little momma's boy," he said, soft, almost a whisper. "There's nothin' down in that cellar but a few daddy long-legs and your own damn boogeymen. Now go get them spuds."

He let go of my shirt and shoved me backwards with his fist, and I stumbled like I always do, my feet being so darn big and my legs so stringy. I landed flat on the floor, and I hurt all over, inside and out. I was crying by then, which added even more to my shame. And I started thinking he was probably right. If I were any kind of a real man, I'd get up on my own two feet and go down there after those spuds, whether I was scared or not.

Lemmy stood up and started laughing and prancing around like a girl. "If it's gonna make you cry and all, honey," he said in a high, fake little voice, *"I'll* go get the dadblamed spuds."

Then I really got mad, because there aren't very many worse things in the world than to have somebody like Lemmy poking fun at you. I don't think I would have done it if I hadn't been so mad, and if I hadn't wanted so much to prove that I wasn't a sissy. Anyway, I got up and grabbed the basket and started wading through the mud to the root cellar.

There I was, out in the sun again, blue sky above, and trees aglitter with dew, just like any other spring morning. Made me feel like I could face almost anything. For a minute or two the world seemed so familiar that I began to whistle and enjoy the feel of the cool mud between my toes. Then, about a stone's throw from the cellar door, I came across another patch of slime, the same as we'd found by the chicken coop.

I squatted down beside it, nearly deaf from the noise of my heart. This slime seemed fresher than the other, and a smell came up from it like from the mouth of a cave that's too dark to see inside of. I stood up slowly, trying not to breathe too fast. My spine felt like ants were marching up it in a long, thick line. Still, I had it in my mind that a man wouldn't run. A man would stay and face whatever came his way.

That's when I heard the sound. It made me think of bees when they swarm in a tree, a thousand little voices raised together to make a single huge and angry one. I looked at the cellar door, and I saw it sort of moving, like there was something big leaning on it, trying to get out all at once. There's a crack between the door and the ground, a couple inches maybe. And through that crack came a mess of gray, wet-looking tuckahoe.

Part of me was still trying to act brave, and it said to me, "Ruben, my boy, you must've eaten something that didn't agree with you, for you are seeing things."

But the rest of me, which was the bigger part, said, "If a fellow can't trust his own eyes, just what *can* he trust?" That bigger part of me didn't give a darn about whether I was brave or a man or not. It just believed what I was seeing and hearing. That's when I dropped the basket and hightailed it for the house.

By the time I came through the front door, I couldn't even talk. I just stood there shaking and sweating, with my mouth going open and shut. I was peeing my pants. I could feel it washing the mud off my feet onto Momma's clean floor, and I didn't even care. She let out a little cry. Pa got up and stared at me. I don't know what he saw in my face but it must have convinced him of something, because I've never seen him look like that before. He was scared, and I know it isn't right, but for just one second I was glad.

Pa grabbed his shotgun from the corner, and he said, "All right, Lemmy. We're gonna go find out what the hell is down there." Then he and Lemmy took off for the root cellar.

Momma got her quilt and she wrapped me up in it and made me sit down on the bench by the fire. She sat beside me, and rocked me and sang to me like she used to do before I got so big. That's all I wanted, just to bury my face in the good clean smells of Momma, and forget there was ever anything else.

We sat like that for a long time, waiting for Pa and Lemmy to come back, watching the sun creep past noon into afternoon and the clouds begin to sweep across the sky again. But Pa and Lemmy never came. And we never heard anything for sure, no roar of the shotgun going off, no terrible screams or cries for help. Once, I fancied I heard a kind of long moan, way off across the straw grass. It could have been the wind, or an owl. But somehow, it made me wonder what we'd do if we had to get away. The only gun in the house besides Pa's ten-gauge was Grampa's Colt pistol, which Pa always kept locked in his trunk. I was pretty sure I could break that lock with a hammer. I was pretty sure I could do a lot of things if it came to saving Momma.

After a time, Momma fell asleep, and I did too, still thinking about that lock. I was just too bone-weary to hold my eyes open anymore. I had a dream, a fine warm dream about fishing down by the river on a summer's day, and when I woke up it took me a minute to remember where I was.

The first thing I noticed was that Momma had left the bench. She was standing beside the front door with a butcher knife in her hands, whispering over and over again, "The Lord helps them that helps themselves. The Lord helps them that helps themselves." All at once, it came to me that there was a funny noise outside, like bees swarming in a tree.

I jumped up, tipping over the bench, and yelled, "Momma! Don't, Momma!"

She turned around and there was a crazy look in her eyes, like I saw once in the eyes of a neighbor woman who stood in the road and watched her house burn down. Momma's face was all shiny with sweat, and that lock of hair had come loose. Oh, how I wanted to tuck it back, and make everything all right. "I won't let it in here, Ruben," she said. "I swear I won't." Before I could get to her, she held up the knife and opened the door.

I stood at the window and screamed. I screamed for a long, long time, even after there was nothing left of Momma but skin and clothes and the butcher knife. No matter how she struck and slashed, the tuckahoe got her anyway. And when it was done, it disappeared under the porch, leaving patches of slime on the wood.

Twilight fell before I came to myself enough to get up and light the lamps. I went in and broke Pa's trunk to pieces with Momma's kitchen hatchet, and got out the Colt and figured out how to load it.

I've been waiting for Pa and Lemmy to come and tell me it was just a mean trick. But now the rain has started in again.

BETWEEN THE WINDOWS OF THE SEA

by Jack Dann

Rita stood at the end of the long, steel pier and stared into the black water below. Waves smashed in below her, the white froth turning to silver in the moonlight. Behind her, past the pier and the bottle-strewn, paper-littered beach, were modern balconied condos and hotels, one indistinguishable from another. A1A and the intersecting streets were quiet, except for the susurration of passing cars. Most of the chic little Soho-style shops were closed; and the college hangouts—the Elbo Room, The Button, Stagger Lee's, Durty Nelly's, and Nards—which had been packed with screaming, drinking students just a few days before, were almost empty. No one was on the beach drinking beer or making love to jangling rock-and-roll music turned up full blast. The large, "ghetto-box" radios had been all the rage, and there had been some talk about outlawing them. But spring break was over and the students were gone. Only their money and bottles and cans and used prophylactics remained behind. Fort Lauderdale was once again left to the locals and the wealthy retirees, to the tourists dressed in flowered shirts and floppy hats, and to the chairman-of-the-board executives and drug merchants who owned million-dollar homes on the intercoastals and whose children spent the long, languorous days cutting screaming wakes in the ocean with their "cigarette" speedboats.

It was cool out tonight, and Rita shivered as she contemplated suicide.

All she had to do was take another step. She could just let the water carry her away. She stared grimly downward at the angry, sudsy water below. No one could find her here. No one could rescue her, scream for her to stop, try to talk her out of it. She was completely alone. The pier was closed, and she'd locked all the doors behind her. The pier contained a restaurant and several overpriced sundry shops. Rita worked as the manager of the restaurant. In reality she was just another waitress, for The Pierpoint was just another diner with a fancy, pretentious name.

She tried to think of something profound to tell herself before she jumped off the pier, but she couldn't think of anything.

Before she could *really* decide if she wanted to do it right now, she jumped into the cold, dark water. It was an icy shock, and then her body became accustomed to it. She had a few seconds of blind panic, then realized that if she changed her mind and decided that she wanted to live after all, she could swim back to shore.

. She swam slowly away from shore, and the undertow, flowing strong below her, helped her, pulling her toward that distant place where the starry sky met the dark ocean. The water now seemed warm as a womb.

Rita was calm. She waited for her life to pass before her as if in a dream, or an old movie—that's what was supposed to happen when you drowned. It was supposed to be a very pleasant experience, really—or so she'd been told. The water carried her along silently, and she bobbed and floated like a marker in her red-and-white, vertical-striped swimsuit. She looked up at the sky, counting the reddish-hued stars, and wondered when *it* was going to happen. But *it* could take hours, she told herself. By then she'd be too far out to swim back. . . .

So what? she asked herself. What else was there for her to do? Go back *there*, back to being a fat waitress in a crumby eat-out, back to her poster-walled little apartment off Commercial Boulevard, where there was nothing to do but watch television reruns or smoke another joint— or worse yet, back to the old hangouts, where bad, yet nostalgic memories were thick as smoke, back to being an over-the-hill '60s love child, a true flower-carrying protester who understood the metaphysical meaning of every one of Bob Dylan's songs . . . ?

Back to being achingly lonely?

I'd rather be dead, she thought.

And no one even *remembers* Bob Dylan anymore. . . .

A dark ocean swell swept over her and she choked, swallowing salty water. She lunged upward, gasping for air, churning the water with her arms, dog-paddling to keep her head as far above the surface as possible.

But the ocean was implacable. It had become cool again, even cold.

It was dark and quiet. Rita looked toward the shore, toward the twinkling, hazy-distant city lights . . . looked over the glassy, undulating surface of the water. She had drifted too far out. She wouldn't be able to swim back.

It was too late!

She panicked, suddenly, desperately wanting to live. She just wanted to feel grass or cement under her feet, look in shop windows, be bored on a Saturday night, chain-smoke nonfilter cigarettes, go to a movie or watch television. Anything but death in an ocean where she could see no bottom, where no one could hear her screams. She tried swimming back to shore, her fleshy arms banging into the water, her short legs kicking, splashing. In moments she was exhausted. She'd never been a good swimmer, certainly not a distance swimmer.

And the water kept carrying her away from the distant shore, as if it were quietly playing with her . . . as if it wanted her. Giving up, she floated—*that* she could do. She could float forever. Floating and waiting to drown, she cried and laughed at herself.

She'd *always* been a phony. Even now . . . especially now. She hadn't *really* expected to die when she jumped into the water. She was play-acting . . . acting out a private fantasy. She was just going to float for a while and then swim back to shore. She'd been a phony hippy, a phony radical, a phony feminist, a phony doper, a phony Protestant, and now a phony suicide.

But the ocean didn't care. It took her warmth and what strength she had. . . .

She started drowning at dawn, which was a rich, hot, ruddy sunrise bleeding into the water, turning blue, then green below. Rita fell asleep again, and inhaled water. She choked and, unable to scream, she kicked and twisted and tried to push herself to the surface, but she hadn't the strength. She felt electric, jolting pain, as if her head would burst. Then gradually the pain receded into darkness. She was falling into what looked like an endless black wall, a huge, curved well of darkness. No memory-movie of her life passed before her.

She passed through the wall into utter blackness.

Then she found herself falling slowly through greenish-gray depths, her arms outstretched as if she were flying. Her eyes were wide, and she could *see*. She tasted salt water, which filled her lungs. Her chest swelled and she exhaled a warm stream of water. She was breathing it. But she didn't need to 'breathe' often; perhaps it was just to satisfy an old autonomic habit.

Rita could see the furrowed ocean bottom far below her, seventy or eighty feet down. For an instant, she experienced acrophobia, for the water was absolutely clear and still. She waved her arms and kicked her feet, testing. She hung midway, floating, slowly turning, free of the past, free of loneliness or emptiness.

Free. . . .

Rita wouldn't accept that she might be dead, or that these, her last thoughts, might be hallucinations, the last, synaptic coursings of a dying mind. She started swimming instead, feeling strong and lean and streamlined and beautiful, sensitive to the private universe of water around her; it was an ever-present pressure against her body, as if a beautiful man with cool skin and fresh breath were pushing against her, entering her. She cut easily through the water like a dolphin.

Sunlight shimmered through the water, turning it blue, which deepened to purple in the depths; but ahead the sea floor rose sharply like underwater crags, turning green, the living green and orange and yellow of a coral reef. Deeper, down the reef's side, the colors became muted, turning almost gray. There was life everywhere. Angelfish seemed to glow yellow and blue through black stripes. Four-eyed butterfly fish seemed to be swimming backward. Summer flounder, shark, and barracuda swam through cliff valleys and narrows; below were anemones and conchs and stars and sponges and long tendrils of seaweed, green against blue.

Rita swam over the reef, diving, as hundreds of tiny silvery fish sparkled all around her, slid past her arms and legs; and the world was color and light and life, every instant filled, as if loneliness and boredom were foreign sounds, words in a language she couldn't remember. She could hear the snapping of shells and a thrumming, a moaning. The ocean was life and sound and color. She could see clearly, as if she were wearing goggles or a face mask. She breathed water and light. She was free of constraint, an exultant ballerina who had conquered gravity.

She rested motionless, drifting downward to land gently upon a smooth, flat spot amid the coral. She stretched, unafraid, even as a huge shadowy manta soared slowly overhead.

She was happy. She had become much more than a client of the sea.

She was home, finally . . . here by the large, rounded coral that looked like French modernist concretion sculpture, by the bony staghorn and rose and soft coral. A school of tiny blue damselfish flittered between mock-stone fronds and coral spikes. She reached out, as if awakening from a perfect dream, to grasp the tiny fish.

Suddenly she felt a sharp pain in her throat. She began to choke. She couldn't *breathe.* She tried to push herself away from the coral, struggled to reach the surface magnified above—an undulating mirror of light that seemed so near.

But the ocean burst into a kaleidoscope of coral color and then, just as quickly, dissolved into complete blackness. . . .

"Hey, are you all right?"

Rita opened her eyes, but everything seemed out of focus, as it used to when she had tried to swim underwater with her eyes open. Then her vision cleared. It was dark, and she was lying on the damp sand of the beach beside the steel pier. The moon was full and had a reddish halo. She shivered—the breeze skimming over the sea carried a northern chill.

"Miss, are you *all right?*"

Disoriented, she looked up at the man kneeling beside her. He was rather handsome, with a full mouth, a cleft chin, and a thin nose that was slightly too long for his squarish face. His thick shock of prematurely gray hair looked blond in the moonlight. Rita tried to sit up, but her body felt heavy and foreign. She leaned into the sand on her elbow and raised her head. Her long, bleached hair was still wet, as was her suit. "How long have I been here?" she asked.

"I don't really know," the man said. "I just came by. I thought something might be wrong."

Rita laughed weakly. "No . . . nothing's wrong."

"Is there anything I can do for you?" Rita shivered, and he took off his jacket and wrapped it around her shoulders. It was sky-blue imitation suede, and warm.

"Thanks," she said, feeling awkward sitting in the sand with this man kneeling beside her. But he *seemed* genuinely interested. Maybe he's just a good Samaritan, she told herself. He certainly wasn't dressed for the beach, not with those white bucks, white, high-waisted slacks that were now crusted with sand, and a starched white shirt that looked bluish in the moonlight. His tie was pulled loose below an open collar.

Rita thought he was beautiful, as cool and crisp as the water.

"Would you care to go and have a drink?" he asked cautiously. "Might warm you up."

"I'm not exactly dressed for it," she said, feeling self-conscious and fat in her sand-sticky swimsuit. She did feel better, though. She could even muse about her suicide attempt. It was as if it had happened to someone else; she felt distanced from it.

But she remembered jumping off the pier, floating out to sea, choking, drowning. She remembered the wall of darkness. She remembered swimming . . . and breathing under water. She could still taste the salty stuff.

"They're really not going to care how you're dressed," the man said. "Not on the strip, anyway. And you can wear my jacket." He seemed in earnest. "Come on, let me help you up."

Easier said than done, she said to herself. But she allowed him to help her to her feet. When she stumbled, he held her close for an instant. She felt dizzy . . . and hungry. It had been quite a while since she'd felt ravenously hungry.

He helped her along as they crossed the beach. Even after they were on the street, he kept his arm around her, his long fingers touching her flabby waist through the material of the jacket he had lent her. They crossed A1A, right on the corner of Las Olas, site of the famous Elbo Room Bar, tourist heaven. The streets were quiet. A few tourists were out. But the students who had been shouting and hanging out and showing off were gone. "Do you want to just stop in here?" he asked, looking into the Elbo Room's window.

"Are you kidding?" she asked, smiling at him—she had a beautiful smile. "It's a trap."

"I vaguely remember it from a long time ago," he said. "Do you know someplace better?"

"Yeah, a little bar down here a ways." They walked toward the intercoastal; in fact a bridge was lifting to let a high-masted sailboat pass under. "You're just visiting, I take it," Rita said. She felt her strength returning.

"I had business in Jacksonville, and I thought that since I was in the neighborhood, so to speak, I'd come back down here for old time's sake. I used to come here for college break." He chuckled. "But that was a *long*, long time ago."

"You must have had some good times. . . ."

"That I did. But I think the real reason I came back was to try to feel the old sensation of being young again . . . you know, the sun all day, the lights and glitter and bars all night. Total freedom, no responsibility." Then, after a pause, he said, "And no money." They both laughed at that. "What about you . . . are you a native?"

"I came down here for spring break too . . . a *long*, long time ago." She smiled. "Only, I stayed."

"Maybe that's what I should have done."

Rita laughed and pointed out the cafe on the other side of the street. It was a gaily painted converted gas station. There were about a dozen outside tables, but only one was occupied, by a young couple sitting close together and sipping wine. They wore identical white shorts and tops. They *had* to be newlyweds. "I have no idea what you do or where you live," Rita said as they crossed the street, "but, believe me, you made the right decision not to stay here."

They sat down at one of the tables, and the waitress, who was about Rita's age, appeared to take their order.

"Hi, how you doin'?" Rita asked.

The waitress looked blankly at her for a second. "You know, you look *so* familiar."

"I'm Rita, from the Pier."

"Well, what can I get you?"

Rita felt herself burning with embarrassment. She'd wanted to impress her new friend, and not even a goddamn local could remember her. She wasn't friends with this waitress, certainly, but they'd seen each other around before. Her companion didn't seem to take any notice. He asked Rita what she wanted—a glass of the house wine and a small chef's salad—and then ordered a Drambuie with a soda on the side for himself. After the waitress left, he finally asked her name.

"Rita . . . Rita Cobia," she replied.

"I'm Stephen Boden from Albany, New York." He grinned. "This whole thing's crazy, isn't it?"

"I guess it is." There was an embarrassing, awkward silence. Rita lowered her eyes and stared at her hands folded on the table.

She *had* tried to kill herself.

She *remembered* drowning.

"Rita . . . ?" Stephen asked. "What were you doing on the beach?"

The waitress came back with drinks and Rita's salad. What she *really* wanted was a hamburger, rare, with a great big Bermuda onion; but that would only bring attention to her weight. After all, fat people eat hamburgers on large, beautiful kemmelwick buns, and skinny people eat chef's salads with oil and vinegar. Heartburn city. . . . Rita took a forkful of meat and lettuce and chewed carefully. "I tried to kill myself last night," she said suddenly, as if she were testing Stephen. "I don't know how I got back on the beach." All that said flatly, matter-of-factly.

Stephen's eyes narrowed. He took another sip of his Drambuie, then followed it with a sip of soda.

"Sounds pretty nutty, huh," Rita said.

"Well . . . I guess it's a good thing I found you."

"It was all over but the chorus by then," and she told him the story, although she was certain that this guy was going to think her a nut case and get away as fast as he could. So what else was new. . . .

"Maybe you blacked out or something and dreamed it and then swam back to shore," Stephen said.

"I was out on the water for a long time," Rita said, musing. "I know that."

"Should I ask why you wanted to kill yourself?"

"If you wanted to relive the old memories, you should've been here last week when the kids were still on the streets," she said, ignoring his question. "But you did say you were down here on business."

"I did, but I guess I really didn't want to come back here until the party was over. I could have changed my schedule around. But the truth is that seeing all those kids would just remind me that I'm too *old* for spring break."

She giggled at that. "What do you do now?" she asked.

"Would you believe real estate?" Stephen seemed relaxed, yet animated; and as he talked to her, he leaned forward as if he were going to whisper, as if everything he had to tell Rita was privileged, secret. Rita found herself doing the same thing; they were blocking out all the noise and activity around them. This was more than just a pickup or a budding friendship. And right now, sitting with Stephen, she felt truly happy. She wouldn't ask for anything more.

"I would believe real estate," Rita said. She was full, and slightly high on the tangy wine.

"This whole place—Lauderdale, the beach, the bars, the sun—represented possibility to me," Stephen continued. "When I first came down here, I thought I could do *anything:* act, become a playwright, a novelist, a screenwriter, a director. I took film in college, which prepared me for absolutely nothing but making films . . . that's another story."

"Did you try to get into films?" Rita asked.

"Not hard enough. I was in advertising for a while, and used some of the stuff I learned in college."

"You didn't like it . . . advertising?"

"Actually, I liked it quite a bit," Stephen said, and he waved to the waitress to bring another round. "Maybe that was the problem. It kept reminding me that I *wasn't* doing film. Close, but no cigar. I'm making more money in real estate, anyway . . . and I'm *real* good at rationalizing. So, glutton for punishment that I am, I came back here to feel what it was like to have it all ahead of me."

"And what does it feel like?"

"I feel good because I'm here with you. But except for meeting you, which made the whole trip worth while, it's been a bust. I should have let well enough alone. I knew this place would look different . . . would be different when seen again through older eyes, but I thought I'd taste *something* of what it used to be like. Yet until now Florida had the same leaden 'feel' of everything else in my life." He laughed harshly. "I guess I've become dried-up and cynical. But what I'm feeling now is the real stuff." He seemed taken aback by that; he leaned backward, as if to think about it. After a long pause he said, "You know, *this* is what it felt like. Just sitting here with you makes me feel like I'm on . . . spring break." He laughed at that, and the harshness disappeared. "I'm starting to sound like a real jerk, aren't I?"

Rita felt her face become warm. "No . . . you're not."

They looked at each other. Rita felt awkward, and Stephen put his hand over hers. She felt her cheeks burn, but she couldn't stop herself from smiling, then giggling. "I'm sorry," she said. "I—"

"I feel the same way," Stephen said. The waitress came back with their drinks, and Stephen paid her. "Let's get out of here and walk around," he continued. "Unless you really want this drink. I feel full of energy; and if I don't walk some of it off, I'm going to be jumping around in my seat like this"—and he jumped up and down and made a silly face. Then he suddenly sat back in his chair. "I'm sorry. I can't believe that I'm trying to get you to take a walk after what you told me. You're probably ready to go home and sleep for forty hours."

"No," Rita said, standing up and leaning forward, reluctant to take her hand out of his. "Let's take a walk."

They walked back to A1A, crossed the street to the beach side and cut through a well-lit parking lot and out onto the cool sand. A few tall palmettos cast long shadows on the beach. They passed a row of cabanas and a painted metal kiosk, where bathers could buy sundries—especially suntan oils—at outrageous prices. Then they walked in the wet sand along the ocean, sidestepping the angled paths of foamy water cutting into the beach.

Rita felt wonderful. Everything around her and Stephen seemed separate and perfect: the sea a darkness, a swelling; the sand seemed almost to glow in the wan moonlight. It was as if all her senses were heightened. She felt as if she were experiencing every smell and sight for the first time. The sea odors were sharp as horseradish and somehow poignant. The waves were a muffled roar, white noise swallowing the city sounds. The breezes were chilly, but the wine she had drunk kept her warm. The sky was a great vault reflected by the sea.

Every moment was magical . . . eternal.

Stephen took her hand. "What about you?"

"What do you mean?"

"You said you came here on college break and stayed."

"That's all there is to tell," Rita said. "I came from a small town in upstate New York, a blinker town."

"A what?"

"You blink, it's gone." He laughed and she continued. "I went to a small college, a religious school. Some friends were coming down here. They talked me into it and here I am."

Stephen didn't press her to speak. They kept walking, giving wide berth to several beached jellyfish in their path.

"My religious education and beliefs were almost the death of me," she said after some time passed. They both giggled and then broke into laughter like nervous high-school students on a first date.

"What do you mean?" Stephen asked.

"Well, this isn't exactly the kind of place a girl with traditional values chooses," Rita said. "I was rebelling, and I suppose it took everyone by surprise when I left the school. I was a good student, didn't get into trouble." There was a strain in her voice. "I'm your typical fat girl."

"You're *not* fat, nor typical, and here you are right in the middle of the sun and sex and drug belt," he said wryly.

"With my morals intact while I tried to off myself by jumping into the ocean." Again they laughed together, but there was a strain. The ocean seemed ominous. "I should have applied for a Guinness world record—I had to be the only sixties hippy, wearing tie-dyed jeans and beads, with my hair down to my ankles practically, who was also a virgin. I can tell you that religious fat girls make poor hippies. I used to sneak off to church. I'd put on my Sunday dress, put my hair up, slather on makeup to make me look middle class and proper, and go to Episcopalian services. I still do it . . . every Sunday."

"Look," Stephen said, stopping, pulling her to a halt too. "You're not skinny, but you're certainly not fat."

"Yes I am, but I've got a pretty face."

He put his arms around her. "When I saw you lying on the beach, I felt like I was eighteen and in love. And that's how I feel right now. . . ."

Rita blushed, not knowing what to say. Against all reason, her instincts were to trust this stranger. She nodded, brushing against his face, which was very close to hers.

They passed a large condo, and then more motels, priced high for the tourists. "I'm staying here," Stephen said, pointing at an old, two-story, white stucco motel. Rita knew of the place. It had a decent reputation, and the new owners had enough taste to do away with the flashing neon and 1950s pink plastic flamingos that had been its trademark for the previous twenty years.

"Why didn't you stay over at the Holiday?"

He grinned. "Over the years I've gotten tired of hassling with desk clerks to get a low floor. So I just go to motels where it's quiet and I can work and it doesn't take an act of bravery to get to my room."

"How do you fly, then?" Rita asked.

"Planes don't bother me . . . only elevators. You know what my shrink told me to do in elevators?" Before Rita could respond, he continued. "He said that every time I get into an elevator, I should force myself to have erotic fantasies. That way, I'd associate elevators with pleasure . . . that was the theory, anyway." He chuckled.

"Did it work?" Rita asked.

"Nah, I'd be too damn nervous and claustrophobic in the elevator to think about sex. In fact, I think it started working the other way around."

"What do you mean?"

"I started getting scared of *sex.*" They both laughed, but there was a nervous tension working between them again. It was palpable, exciting. . . .

"Well, maybe we should give the elevator another chance," Rita said, surprised at herself.

They went to Stephen's room and turned on all the lights, as if they were both afraid of the dark; then they sat down on the large brown Naugahyde couch that faced sliding glass doors which opened onto a private patio. They looked out onto the beach but could see only reflections of the room in the glass. They joked and talked and became nervously silly.

When they ran out of small talk, Rita made the first move. She leaned against him, made herself vulnerable to him. There was a moment of shyness and awkwardness, as he began to caress and kiss her, exploring gently, as if searching for something precious that had been lost long ago. Passion was gradual, a soft falling, then a quickening. Rita felt as if she had two selves: one, who was burning . . . or choking, drowning; and another, who watched coolly, curiously, as if from a distance. Rita felt no shame, nor was she nervous; but Stephen got up and turned off all the lights, bringing the sand and sea outside the sliding doors into their private world.

Rita helped him remove her suit. But when he was ready to enter her, she pulled him away from the couch and led the way outside onto the damp sand.

"Someone might see us," he whispered, yet he didn't insist, for the beach was empty. They were hidden in shadow . . . hidden by the world. The sea was a dark, living thing before them, murmuring, speaking in a language just beyond sense. The moon was clear, a round white lantern turning the fine sand to opal.

Rita held Stephen close and looked up at the sky, as if studying the stars. She moaned softly, felt a bright flash of pain as he entered her. She could hear his labored breathing as if it were the surf pounding on top of her. His mouth locked on hers. Everything became liquid and slippery and clean. It was like washing . . . like swimming . . . like breathing water.

She awoke to his soft breathing beside her. She lay quietly and felt a strength, a muscular tightness throughout her body. She felt long and thin and beautiful. It was still dark; she couldn't have slept for more than an hour.

Stephen curled against her, murmured something in his sleep, and pressed his face into her breast. His tangled hair tickled her nut-brown shoulder. She giggled, feeling pleasure wash over her again. She caressed him, exploring. He felt as cool as the sea to the touch. He smelled as tangy and salty as the soapy whitecaps washing and smoothing over the sand.

She felt completely awake, alive, full of energy.

It was then she heard the sea. Amid its muted pounding and breaking and susurration, it seemed to speak to her . . . call to her. She could almost make out its words.

The sea wooed her with whisperings, and Rita found herself answering. Making love to Stephen had been a celebration, but now she wanted to go home.

Feeling the pull of the sea as if she were in its undertow, she kissed Stephen good-bye. She felt an instant of nostalgic regret, and then she stood up naked and ran toward the ocean. She took long strides, felt her scalp tingle as her long hair blew in the salty breeze, felt her body as her own, not as an ugly object worn like an oversized coat.

She jumped into the surf, which was refreshing and as cool as Stephen as he slept. She ran through the shallow water, lifting her legs high, splashing, and then swam. She was strength itself. She was a flowing. She cut through the sea like a fish sojourning from the deep.

The ocean was cool and patient and enveloping. It claimed her, as had Stephen. It breathed. It entered her. It pulled her down into its living stillness.

And once again, Rita took a deep breath . . . and became smooth and thin, formed by the sea.

THE BATTERING

by Steve Rasnic Tem

They stopped at a diner in Georgia. It was all chrome, fifties style, and it sat on the edge of a pine forest. That's what had appealed to Jack. The forest, for some reason, made him feel safer.

There were only two or three customers, but Jack still ushered Lisa to the booth farthest from the counter. One exit was close at hand, and it would be a short run to the car. Jack stationed himself between Lisa and the rest of the diner, trying to pretend no one else was there, not even the waitress. As far as these people were concerned, he and Lisa were just travelers, tourists, passing through.

The waitress started over with two menus. Jack held his breath. She smiled when she handed Lisa hers, mumbled something like "pretty little girl," and Jack relaxed a little.

"I'll be back . . ." The waitress stopped, looking at her arms, down at her feet, as if an insect were bothering her. She rubbed at an upper arm. "Sorry." She shook her head. "I'll be back in just a bit for your order."

The waitress walked away, nervously playing with the long curl hanging over her ear. Jack glanced at Lisa, who was busy studying the menu, oblivious to everything else. It had always amazed him how easily she went inside like that.

"Daddy, what's 'creeps'?"

"That's pronounced 'crepe,' honey. It's like a thin pancake, with eggs in it. Try it; I think you might like it."

"Naw, I'll just have a hamburger with chili sauce."

"That's it? For breakfast?"

"Yep!" She giggled. He normally would have shown her that he appreciated her little joke, but Jack was finding it impossible to smile.

The waitress was back in only a few minutes. She seemed agitated. She stood near Jack, staring down at her pad. "Your order?"

"Oh, yeah. Crepes for me, I guess. And coffee."

"And the girl?" The waitress jerked her head toward Lisa, without looking at her.

Lisa stared at the waitress. "Do you have tomato juice?"

The waitress would not look up. Jack watched her, watched her fingers clench themselves white on the pad, and felt himself lean toward Lisa. He wanted to tell her not to ask questions. He wanted to shout at her, order her to shut up. "Of course, of course," the waitress mumbled.

"Well, I'll have that." Lisa was giggling. "And a hamburger!" She started laughing.

"Fine," the waitress said shortly, and reached to pull Lisa's menu away from her. Jack had a feeling, and tried to reach the menu first, but he was too late.

The waitress had Lisa by the hand, Lisa's small fingers still pinching the menu, and the waitress was squeezing, squeezing. Lisa's mouth gaped open.

Jack jumped up and pulled the waitress away, then slung Lisa under his arm, started racing toward the door.

As he hit the door bar, the waitress was screaming. By the time he reached the car, the cook and the other customers were hurrying out, coming for them, coming for Lisa.

Jack and Elaine had always wanted a boy. When Lisa came, however, it was fine with Jack. She was the most beautiful baby he had ever seen, and it was a thrill to watch her grow, developing right before his eyes into a beautiful little girl. Elaine wasn't so sure. She kept a distance from the child. At first Jack thought it was just that she wanted a boy so badly. In fact, he was so drawn to Lisa he couldn't imagine anyone else feeling differently. It would have seemed crazy to him.

But then Elaine started voicing her complaints. "Things haven't been the same between us since Lisa came." Elaine had taken up smoking; Jack thought it was a disgusting habit. He didn't enjoy the taste of his wife's lips anymore.

"I could probably get used to your smoking, Elaine. But I've been

watching you—you smoke the most when you're with Lisa. It's like you
. . . subconsciously *want* to make her sick."

Elaine laughed harshly. "Oh, you're something. You can't say anything directly. You have to use words like 'subconscious' and 'uninten-
tional.' Why don't you just spit it out?"

"I think you hate her! I think you can't stand to be around her, and
she's just a *baby!*"

She turned her back, knowing that would aggravate him even more.
She was always turning her back when they talked about Lisa.

"I'm not the only one," she said quietly.

Jack reached over and grabbed her arm. She squirmed away from
him. "Just what is that supposed to mean?"

Elaine sighed heavily and shrugged her shoulders. He wondered
when she had become such a martyr; overnight, it seemed to him.
"You're so blind, Jack," she said. "You don't notice a damn thing you
don't want to!" She stopped, moved toward the couch.

"Go on," he said. "Don't just walk away."

She sat down and stared at her cigarette. With a sudden expression
of disgust she smashed it out in a huge ashtray almost overflowing with
broken butts. "None of the other kids in the neighborhood can stand
her. Oh, they like her fine at first. She's a cute kid, and she laughs a lot.
Kids like that, I guess." She frowned and laughed at herself. The gesture appalled him, he could see so much self-loathing in it. "But after a
while, just a week or two, sometimes just a couple of days, they can't
stand to be around her. Most of the time they just walk away. Sometimes they hit her, or shove her down."

Jack thought about the bruises on Lisa's arms and legs. She said
she'd gotten them playing. Jack had always suspected that Elaine had
had something to do with them. "She's never said anything."

Elaine was rubbing her face, too hard. "I know. It's like she doesn't
even notice, or doesn't care."

"But *why* wouldn't they like her? She's a sweet little girl." He
watched Elaine rubbing her face to a bright red. "How can I believe
that, Elaine? You don't like her, so how do I know you're not just
distorting what you see?"

Elaine's hands were shaking. "You *bastard.* You're the *only* one
around here who doesn't know. The neighbors won't even let her into

their homes anymore. They won't say why, they just make up some weird excuse. I swear, you're just as dumb as she is."

Suddenly Jack found himself standing over her, his hand raised, the fingers curling into a fist. "Take it back! Don't you ever talk about her that way again."

Elaine smiled at him stupidly. "Go ahead, hit me, Jack. Hit me just as hard as you can. Then maybe you won't ever have to punch your precious little girl."

Jack stood there shaking. Then he turned around, almost running to the door. "Bitch!" he shouted, once, struggling for breath. He knew he was quite capable of hitting her again and again until he was exhausted from it. That new self-knowledge was infuriating.

"Daddy, I'm hungry." Lisa curled up on the passenger side, pulling her small, naked doll up against her face vigorously.

"I know, honey. Me, too. We'll find a grocery store and I'll go in and get us something."

"Can't I go in too?"

Her ability to ignore what was happening to them amazed him. He'd talked to her about it, but she didn't seem to have the slightest idea what was going on. "Not this time, honey. Don't you remember? I know you don't understand it; I don't understand it either. But it's dangerous."

Lisa nodded drowsily. In moments the naked doll was bobbing up and down in the rhythms of her sleep.

Jack watched her: she looked normal, *super*-normal in her sleep. This thing, this energy she had, was draining her. He didn't understand the specifics, but somehow it made perfect sense to him.

He had no idea where he was going. North, somewhere, then maybe west. At times he thought about getting them plane tickets out of the country. Crazily, he hoped she wouldn't have this effect on foreigners. But he was afraid of the two of them being trapped in an enclosed space like that. There was no way he could fight off a planeful of passengers, even if he was able to sneak a gun on board.

He felt the pistol tucked into the holster beneath his left arm. He wondered if the jacket concealed it all that well. It was craziness; he knew nothing about guns. The morning before they'd left Florida, he'd broken into his neighbor's apartment. The man was an idiot, always showing the thing off, explaining how carefully he had hidden it.

But it did feel oddly reassuring. Whether Jack thought he could ever use it or not.

He was experimenting now. With Lisa's life and his own. There was nothing particularly magical about his leaving Florida, but he had no idea what might work, if anything. Lisa was born in Florida, so maybe the power would decrease the farther she was away from Florida. It made a kind of skewed sense. Just as what she'd been born with made a kind of skewed sense.

Jack watched his daughter sleeping. She seemed so powerless. Like a doll. He still remembered what life had been like for him at that age; he always would. The adults in your life could do whatever they wanted to you. He used to think that once he got older he would have his vengeance.

"I'm sorry, Lisa! I didn't *mean* to. It was an accident. I didn't do anything *wrong.*"

By the time Jack had reached the dining room, the screams had stopped. Elaine was on the floor by the dining-room table, clutching Lisa in her arms. Blood-streaked arms; Lisa's forehead was a bloody mess. Lisa cried softly, too softly for so much blood.

"What happened?" He wanted to shout it, but his voice came out a whisper.

Elaine rocked Lisa, trying to comfort her, trying to stop her tears. She cooed to her, as if this were not her damaged child, but a newborn, fresh out of the womb. And bloody as all newborns.

Lisa's eyes were closed in pain. Blood clotted her eyelashes and eyebrows. Jack thought he was going to cry too.

Elaine *was* crying, in a singsong, almost a scream, as she rocked Lisa.

"How did it happen?" He tried to raise his voice above Elaine's cries.

"I . . . I just turned my *head!* That was *all!* It was like she *dived* for the edge of the table." Elaine gasped, trying to catch her breath.

That gave Lisa a chance to speak. "Why did you *do* that, Mommy? Why did you *hurt* me?" Lisa had opened her blood-clotted lids. She was beautiful. She had a doll's beautiful blue eyes.

"But I didn't. Jack, I swear." Elaine looked panicked, sick. "I didn't do it, honey. You *fell,* but I . . . really don't understand how." She turned back to Jack, pulling Lisa more tightly against her chest. "I had her balanced on my knees. Her little feet went up on tiptoe on top of my knees. She was fine; I just looked away for a *second.* I felt her body bend, then get tense. Like she was jumping. It was as if she dived for the edge of the table."

"Elaine." Jack knew he was staring at his wife, but he couldn't stop himself. "You're saying she did this to herself on purpose."

"Jack, are you thinking . . ."

"No, I don't think you did it. I know I've been suspicious, but I never thought you'd do anything like this. I know you didn't try to hurt her."

"It was like she dived, Jack . . ."

"Oh, Mommy! Oh, Mommy, it hurts so bad!" Lisa buried her face in Elaine's neck, spreading the blood over her mother's mouth and chin. Jack watched Elaine's teeth and tongue rubbing at the blood, worrying her lip. He rarely heard Lisa call Elaine Mommy.

"Oh, Lisa, I'm sorry," she sobbed. "I'm so sorry!"

Jack looked away. He could see Lisa diving through the air, her arms outstretched into a perfect swan.

A week later Elaine left them both. They hadn't heard from her since.

In North Carolina, Jack left Lisa sleeping in the car while he went inside a grocery store for food. Fresh sandwiches were available in the deli department, and small cartons of milk. He got Lisa chocolate. He figured several bags of fruit, fig bars, and raisins would do awhile for the snacks.

When he got outside the store an old man was leaning over the passenger-side window of the car, peering inside.

"Get away from that car!" Jack dropped the groceries and ran across the parking lot, grabbed the old man's shoulder, spun him around. The old man's eyes were white, his lips fat and raw. "What are you doing here?"

"Shouldn't leave her like that . . . might hurt somebody, that one."

Jack pushed him away. Blood was smeared around the top of the window. He examined the rubber seal—two fingernails had been jammed in, torn out. When he turned back, the old man was licking his fingers, tending to their torn and bleeding tips.

The sandwiches tasted good. Jack glanced down to see his daughter munching greedily on the fruit. He avoided looking at the glass above her; he'd smeared it badly trying to clean it.

He'd always thought that he and Elaine would make good parents. It had been essential to him that they be good parents. That was another thing you did when you were small and defenseless—you decided you'd be very different when you grew up. You'd get revenge on the adults who'd mistreated you, and at the same time you'd be a different kind of parent. *I'll never do that to my kids.*

Lisa was his sweet little girl. Sometimes her petiteness amazed him. She was constructed like a doll; it made her seem almost unreal at times.

Just as their lives had become unreal. The *unfairness* of it disturbed him the most. That she should be a target like this, even to people they'd never met before. It reminded Jack of all the other unfairnesses of childhood, and being told by adults, with a bizarre sort of pride, that life itself was unfair.

Sure, he'd been beaten as a child, locked in closets, burned with cigarettes, marked with a knife. He didn't think too much about the specifics; they all too quickly became a boring, bathetic litany of horrors. It was the injustice that he remembered, the rage. The feeling he'd get when he read comic books, that if he could just turn all that injustice and rage into a rare and mystical power, he could turn whole cities to dust.

Lisa was playing quietly with her doll again, oblivious to their difficulties. She always refused to put clothes on the doll, said she liked it better this way. Children were survivors. Jack himself had survived. He and Elaine had done okay with Lisa. She didn't seem damaged.

Actually, what had seemed most unfair was the fact that Jack's parents were such ordinary people. His mother kept a nice house. His father was a respected small-town lawyer. His parents argued, but not any more than others'.

Jack just didn't do things right. It always came down to that. He had a younger brother, Billy, who always seemed to do everything right. "Billy's the kind of boy I like," he heard his father tell a neighbor one time. "He does everything I want him to do."

They stopped once to catch some sleep. Jack pulled off into a wooded area just across the Virginia border. It felt good to curl up with his daughter in his arms. Her soft breathing against his neck. She made him feel better, made some of the pain go away.

"You know it makes me mad when you cry like that," his mother used to say. "But you just keep on and on."

The painted features on Lisa's doll had worn off a long time ago. For some reason, that pleased her. She got her colored marking pens out and made new faces for the doll, a new one almost every week. It pleased her that she could make it wear any face she wanted. She gave it large eyes, a small nose, mouth a dark grim line. It had accidents, livid red wounds and blackened eyes, that sometimes took weeks to heal, that sometimes got worse. And after she'd rubbed the markings away you could see ghost impressions of the wounds. Every night before bed, Lisa made sure the doll wore a long black smile.

"Now, you listen to me, Missy. You're doing this on purpose!" Jack had almost fallen asleep at the wheel. He realized it was Lisa's high-pitched scolding that brought him around. "It's your *own* fault they hurt you!"

She was scarring the doll's face vigorously up and down with the red marker, virtually obliterating its features.

"I assure you something like this has never happened before in our school, Mr. West. Miss Reynolds is a fine teacher, one of our finest. And I know it won't happen again."

Jack wasn't reassured, and he had no desire to talk to Lisa's principal in any case. Like many heads of institutions, her main roll was that of apologist for the staff, while pretending to give clients' complaints a sympathetic ear. He'd seen enough of it over the years; adults loved to apologize for each other. It was as if they had to believe that everyone was well-meaning, and democratically equal in ability and honor.

He turned to Miss Reynolds, who sat slumped in a chair, one hand nervously brushing at a temple, as if to rub evidence out of her thoughts. "You slapped my daughter, Miss Reynolds," he said simply.

"I know. I feel terrible about it. It . . . it's difficult to explain." She twisted her hands together in a painful-looking contortion. Jack looked away.

"Look, I'm not trying to bulldoze you here. I'm not threatening a lawsuit. And I don't think you're a terrible person. I just want to know exactly what happened between you and my daughter."

That seemed to make a difference. If anything, Miss Reynolds appeared overly anxious to unburden herself.

"Lisa is basically a *lovely* child," she began. "Almost doll-like." She paused, as if she realized she wasn't getting to the point. "But she has a certain—stubbornness, I guess. You don't realize it at first; it's very subtle. But after a while you realize that she's been doing just about whatever she pleases, and when you catch her, and give her a consequence, she's terribly apologetic and, well, really *too* hard on herself about it. But then, first thing you know it, she's back doing the same thing again. Punishments just won't work for her; it's like she wants them."

Jack nodded. "Could you be more specific? It's hard to know what you're getting at."

"I'm constantly telling her not to play with the blocks during reading group. But, every day, she gets up from her group table and walks over to the toy bin and gets them out. Then she sits down on the floor—she doesn't play with them, just holds them. As if she were just waiting for me to punish her."

"And what's the usual punishment?"

"Oh, time out in the corner. But first thing I know, she's back at the toy box, sitting on the floor, the blocks in her hand. I'll take away her recess time, or give her work to do, or try to distract her with another task. Nothing has ever worked. She says she's sorry; she says she's a bad person. Then she goes and does it again. Then sits there unmoving, like an old rag doll or something."

"What happened today?"

"I . . . I suppose I was tired. I have this cold; I didn't get much sleep last night. But I'm not making excuses; I know what I did was inexcusable. She'd been doing the thing with the blocks all day. So I thought I'd try ignoring her. It worked for a while; she didn't know what to do. But then she started bringing over the blocks, dropping them into my lap. Then *I* didn't know what to do. I moved her back to the corner, rather roughly, I'm afraid, and ordered her to sit still. This time, she went back to the toy box, got the blocks, walked back to where I was conducting the reading group and dropped them on me again. Then *stood* there, *waiting* for me to punish her. I knew she'd found a new way, a new variation to get to me. Something happened to me then—I knew I couldn't teach like that."

Jack said very little the rest of the conference. He was careful to thank Miss Reynolds for being honest with him, and tried to say as little to the principal as possible. But the principal did manage to say one thing that got to him, in her condescending attempts to be nice and complimentary.

"She *is* a lovely child, Mr. West. A doll. She takes after her father." She chuckled. "She's just like a tiny version of you."

Jack decided to find a hotel room in Indianapolis. They were both too tired to think straight, and Lisa seemed delirious at times. She had a cough, and he detected a little bit of fever. That scared him more than anything, because how could he dare take her to a doctor?

Rest might fix quite a few things. Besides, he needed the time to think. Stray ideas and images nagged him, but refused to fall into place.

It was a large hotel downtown. Jack paid for the room, momentarily leaving Lisa asleep in the car. He had parked in the hotel lot, at what he considered a safe distance from the other cars.

Then he ran back to the car and took Lisa up the back staircase. He had her wrapped in a blanket, only her arm hanging out, which still clutched the doll covered with the colored markings, mutilated cartoon-fashion.

There was no one in the corridor, so slipping her into the room was easy.

Elaine and Jack had had big plans for their little girl. She'd have ballet lessons, piano lessons, nothing but the best. All the things they had never had.

And Jack would treat her the way his parents had never treated him. She was his little doll; he couldn't love her too much.

Lisa had a power like no one had ever seen before. It terrified people, shook them out of their complacency. Made them realize they were not the nice, well-meaning, normal people they thought they were.

As a child, Jack had wanted power, wanted to turn his rage into a magic that would make them all sorry they had been so unfair to him.

It wasn't his fault. Even when he did things he knew he'd be punished for, it wasn't his fault. Even when he did something and sat there waiting for them to beat him like some weakling, some passive rag doll, it wasn't his fault. They didn't have to accept the invitation.

Now his own daughter had power, and surely there was something Jack could do with it. Make it work to their advantage. He just had to figure things out.

Lisa had smeared color on her fingers, her arms, her face. Like theatrical makeup, making her cheeks and mouth and eyes look as if they were bleeding.

Jack took the doll and dropped it on the floor. It gazed up at him, eyeless now, forehead and sockets and cheeks blended together with crimson. He propped Lisa's head up on the pillow. Then he went into the bathroom.

He was soaking a washrag for Lisa's face when he first heard the rumbling. It sounded like thunder, but Jack remembered that the sky was clear.

He lathered the rag carefully with soap. The thunder was in the hall. He lathered and lathered until the pink washrag was almost completely white. There was a pounding of many fists and a scratching of many frenzied fingers and a screeching of a multitude of hysterical throats at their door.

He had to use plenty of soap; Lisa had so much color on her. And that wasn't good for her. His beautiful daughter was a doll, his doll, and her skin was extremely delicate.

When the crashing and tearing began in the next room, the sounds so like animal sounds but still so human, so adult, Jack almost turned to see what was happening. He was crazy to think hiding her would work. Whatever she had was strong enough to draw them to the room. He didn't turn to see what was happening. He couldn't. He could not bring himself to walk into the bedroom, to see what all those adult fists and nails and teeth were doing to his beautiful little girl. Instead, he began thinking of numbers, arithmetic. He started wondering how many guests a hotel of this size could hold, and how many of them could fit into that one little room, taking turns, fighting each other in their mystical need to get to that small broken form on the bed. And soon he could no longer wonder at all. Soon he could scarcely think.

He had to get the rag just right, the right amount of soap, and just the right temperature. He'd always wanted to be the perfect parent. He loved Lisa very much. And it must have worked out; she was so well-behaved. Even now; her love for him filled him with such satisfaction, the sense that all wrongs had been righted. Vengeance had finally occurred. Such power. Such good behavior.

She hadn't even cried.

THE SHADOW OF A HAWK

by Nina Kiriki Hoffman

Trudging through the slushy aftermath of an East Coast winter, Merle felt cold shoot through her, a jolting lance of it, aimed at her heart. She stopped in the shadow of the campus chapel and checked the black buttons on her dark gray coat. All of them were fastened. How had the cold reached her? She glanced skyward, at a distant sun, a pale blister in the dull gray skin of clouds. At her feet, the last moldering leaves from the fall before still edged the cement walk, black and slippery in the slush. The air was wet; the scent of sewage carried even this far, all the way to High Street. And then she caught the warm, friendly smell of pipe tobacco.

Merle glanced behind her. One of the professors; she could identify him by the leather patches on the elbows of his loose beige sweater. He was walking away from her, trailing a streamer of pipe smoke. He must have just stepped out of the chapel.

Merle stood, her fake-fur-lined rubber boots planted firmly on the slick walk, and watched him, trying to trigger his awareness with the strength of her gaze. Stop. Turn. See her, she sent to him in silence. But he ambled on without a backward glance.

It was only later, after she had climbed the three flights of stairs, slipped into her tiny apartment, peeled the gloves off her numbed fingers and put the kettle on for tea that she wondered. Why had she tried to attract his attention? Usually she walked with her eyes downcast, creating her own island of impenetrability wherever she went. Extend a peninsula to the mainland of humanity and things could invade; she had learned that, early.

And: how had a blast of cold air come *out* of the chapel?

She thought she saw him again in the cafeteria at lunch the next day. She had three pints of milk and an orange on her tray. Everything else at the counter had repulsed her. She propped an open book on her bulging pouch of a purse and ignored the other people sitting down at one end of the table. Sipping milk through a straw, Merle began to bury herself in the mystery novel in front of her, waiting for all the people to be explained and their motives dissected by the detective. A gasp startled her out of the book. She looked up, for a moment disoriented in the room where background music and incessant chatter seemed to mix with smoke to haze everything in confusion. "You mean, it got out of the genetic engineering lab?" asked one person of another in a hushed voice. "They haven't told the press, have they?"

Merle put one hand up to her face and then peered out over her thumb at the couple sitting across from each other down the table.

"Not so loud," said the man. "It's the lab strain of *E. coli*. It's been bred for years in isolation and under special conditions. It'll probably die in the outside world."

The woman looked down at her tray of half-eaten food, then looked at her hands, turning them back and forth, holding them close to her face. "I feel sick," she said.

Merle sipped her milk, the thick cool white spreading over her tongue, sliding down her throat. She glanced about and saw her professor, his head haloed by pipe smoke. His hair clustered in soft brown curls over his head. His eyes were pale blue, lambent in the smoky light, and he had a mustache. His nose was straight and long, and his lower lip was full. He reminded Merle of an English professor she had once had, the one who taught the Romantic Poets. He sat alone.

Merle stared at him.

For an instant he looked back, his brows lifting. He took his pipe out of his mouth and blew smoke toward her.

Merle lowered her eyes, focused on her book. She put her hands up to cover her ears, cupping her hair under her palms. For a moment, out of all the smells in the cafeteria, she caught a whiff of pipe tobacco, and she knew they had shared something more intimate than gazes. She was breathing air he had breathed. She crossed her arms over her stomach and hugged herself.

Only a handful of people showed up for sociology class the next morning. Merle stared down at the cuff buttons on her black sleeves, studied her pale, slender hands. She had laid them flat across her sociology text. They contrasted sharply with its dark red-brown cover. Between her hands, a sandstone statue looked out of the cover, its irisless eyes seeming to peer over her left shoulder.

Merle sat in the back of the tall, still room. She looked up. Between her and the other students, who all sat up front that day, lay volumes of venetian-blind-striped gray light, broken by the upthrust of black, gray and brown plastic desk chairs. She stared at the backs of the others' heads. Even the blonde's hair washed out in this light, looking ashy. On the blackboard behind the podium, a linked chain of eraser claps lay faintly, chalk spread around the darker rectangles like spores cast from ripe mushrooms onto black paper.

Five minutes after the hour, a sour-faced secretary came in. "Sociology 105 canceled," she wrote on the board.

"Why?" asked one of the students.

"Your professor is ill," said the secretary, tight-lipped. She left.

"Everybody's sick," said one of the students to another. "I think it's this new flu. Half my hall stayed in bed this morning. My own roommate—"

"Don't breathe on me," said the girl, turning away from him. She uttered a short, flattened laugh. No one laughed with her.

The others left. Merle opened her textbook and began reading about rites of passage.

The next morning, she was the only one who came to class. The long, cool, green halls had seemed deserted as she walked them, her boots sounding like slaps on the gray-green tiles, the noise preceding her, following her, returning to her. The bells didn't ring, but the large, round, white-faced clocks still ran. She slid into her back-row seat and waited as the red second hand swept around the clock, accruing minutes in its wake. After a while she opened her text and stared down at a page, but her eyes didn't focus; she was only aware of a lace of black print on eggshell white, with two blocks of highlighter blue.

" 'I have been half in love with easeful Death,' " said a voice.

Merle looked up. Her professor stood at the podium, his pipe in his hand.

He smiled. "Let's discuss instinctive behavior," he said.

Merle took out her pen and opened her notebook.

"It's a documented fact that when a hawk flies over a hen yard, the chickens will run for cover. In fact, you don't even need a real hawk. A silhouette will send them running, and this is true even of chickens raised in isolation, who aren't familiar with other members of their own species.

"How do you suppose that's possible?" he continued. "Isn't that a wonderful thing, that somewhere, printed on a chicken's genes, is the wisdom to flee from even the shadow of a hawk?"

Merle looked up at him. She set her pen down. She licked her lip.

"You know how that's possible, amazing as it is, unlikely as it is?" he said. He leaned over the podium and smiled at her. "It's because the chickens that don't run from the shadow of a hawk get eaten before they can reproduce. Evolution is so elegant. It borders on the magical, don't you think?"

Her feet felt cold. Merle put a hand to her stomach, feeling a faint churn of nausea. She touched her lips, then blinked. The professor had disappeared.

She rose and put on her coat, lapping one edge over the other. She felt so cold, suddenly, so cold and sick. She could feel sweat forming on her forehead. She walked to a window, jerked on a string to lift the blinds, opened the window and leaned out.

When she had finished being sick, she peered at the sky from eyes swimming with tears. A large shadow against the pale spring blue, but it was being pursued and harassed by two small shadows. Merle rubbed her eyes and looked. A hawk, beleaguered by jays.

"Not everyone is a chicken," she whispered.

But she felt so terribly cold.

TOY

by Bill Pronzini

It was Jackey who found the toy, on a Saturday afternoon in mid-July.

Mrs. Webster was in the kitchen when he came home with it. "Look at this, Mom," he said. "Isn't this neat?"

She looked. It was an odd gray box, about the size of a cigar box; Jackey lifted its lid. Inside were a score or more of random-shaped pieces made out of the same funny-looking material as the box. It seemed to be some sort of slick, shiny plastic, only it didn't really look like plastic. Or feel like plastic when she ran her finger over the lid.

"What is it, Jackey?"

"I dunno. Some kind of model kit, I think."

"Where did you get it?"

"Found it, in the vacant lot by the Little League field. I was hunting lost balls. It was just lying there under a bunch of leaves and junk."

"Well, someone must have lost it," Mrs. Webster said. "I suppose we'll have to put an ad in the Lost and Found."

"Maybe nobody'll claim it," Jackey said. "I'm going to put it together, see what it is."

"I don't think you should . . ."

"Oh, come on, Mom. I won't use glue or anything. I just want to see what it is."

"Well . . . all right. But don't break anything."

"I don't think you *can* break this stuff," Jackey said. "I dropped the box on the way home, right on the sidewalk. It landed on its edge and didn't even get a scratch."

He went upstairs with the toy. Mrs. Webster had no doubt that he would be able to fit the pieces of the model together; for a boy of twelve, he had a remarkable engineering aptitude.

And he *did* fit the pieces together. It took him two hours. Mrs. Webster was out on the back porch, putting new liner on the pantry shelves, when she heard the first banging noise—low and muffled, from up in Jackey's room. A minute later there was another one, and a minute after that, a third. Then Jackey yelled for her to come up. The fourth bang, exactly a minute after the third, sent her straight to his room.

The box and the assembled toy were sitting on Jackey's "workbench," the catchall table his father had built for him. What the toy most resembled, she thought, was a cannon; at least, there was a round barrel-like extremity with a hole in it, set at an upward angle to the model's squarish base. She was sure it was a cannon moments later, when it made the banging noise again and a round, gray, pea-sized projectile burst out of it and arced two thirds of the way across the room.

"Neat, huh?" Jackey said. "I never saw one like this before."

"Cannons," Mrs. Webster said, and shook her head. "I don't like that sort of toy. I don't like you playing with it."

"I'm not. It sort of works by itself."

"By itself?"

"I don't even know where those cannonballs come from. I mean, *I* didn't put 'em in there."

"What *did* you do, then?"

"I didn't do anything except stick the pieces together the way I thought they ought to go. When I snapped the barrel on, something made a funny noise down inside the base. Next thing, it started shooting off those little balls."

It shot off another one just then, and the projectile—slightly larger than the last one, Mrs. Webster thought—went a foot farther this time. An uneasiness formed in her. She didn't like the look of the model cannon or whatever it was. Toys like that . . . they shouldn't be put on the market.

"You dismantle that thing right now," she said. "You hear me, Jackey? And be careful—it might be dangerous."

She went downstairs. But the banging noise came again, and again after exactly one minute. Each seemed a little louder than the last. The second one brought her back to the foot of the stairs.

"Jackey? I thought I told you to dismantle that thing."

Bang! And there was a thud, a crash from inside Jackey's room.

"What was that? What are you doing up there?"

Silence.

"Jackey?"

"Mom, you better come in here. Quick!"

She hurried up the stairs. There was another bang just as she reached the door to Jackey's room, followed by the sound of glass breaking. She caught the knob, jerked the door open.

She saw Jackey first, cowering back alongside the bed, his eyes wide and scared. Then she saw the far wall, opposite the workbench—the dents in the plasterboard, the jagged hole in the window, the projectiles on the floor ranging from pea-sized to apricot-sized. And then she saw the toy. Chills crawled over her; she caught her breath with an audible gasp.

The model had grown. Before, less than five minutes ago, it had been no larger than a small model tank; now it was three times that size. It had subtly changed color, too, seemed to be glowing faintly now as if something deep inside it had caught fire.

"Jackey, for God's sake!"

"Mom, I couldn't get near it, I couldn't touch it. It's *hot*, Mom!"

She didn't know what to do. She started toward Jackey, changed her mind confusedly and went to the workbench instead. She reached out to the toy, then jerked her hand back. Hot—it gave off heat like a blast furnace.

Oh my God, she thought, it's radioactive—

Bang!

A projectile almost as large as a baseball erupted from the toy's muzzle, smashed out the rest of the window and took part of the frame with it. Jackey yelled, "Mom!" but she still didn't know what to do. She stared at the thing in horror.

It had grown again. Every time it went off it seemed to grow a little bigger.

That's not a toy, that's some kind of weapon . . .

Bang!

A projectile just as large as a baseball this time. More of the window frame disappeared, leaving a gaping hole in the wall. From outside, Mrs. Webster could hear the Potters, their neighbors to the north, shouting in alarm. For some reason, hearing the Potters enabled her to act. She ran to where Jackey was crouched, caught hold of his arm, pulled him toward the door.

On the workbench, the gray thing was the size of a portable TV set. She thought she could see it pulsing as she and Jackey stumbled out.

Bang!

Bang!

On the street in front, she stood hugging Jackey against her. He was trying not to cry. "I didn't mean to do anything, Mom," he said. "I didn't *mean* it. I only wanted to see how it worked."

Bang!

Flames shot up from the rear of the house, from the back yard: the big oak tree there wore a mantle of fire. People were running along the street, crowding around her and Jackey, hurling frightened questions at them.

"I don't know," she said. "I don't *know!*"

And she was thinking: Where did it come from? How did it get here? Who would make a monstrous thing like that?

Bang!

Bang!

BANG!

The projectile that blew up the Potters' house was the size of a cantaloupe. The one a few minutes later that destroyed the gymnasium two blocks away was the size of a basketball. And the one a little while after that that leveled the industrial complex across town was the size of a boulder.

The thing kept growing, kept on firing bigger and bigger projectiles. By six o'clock that night it had burst the walls of the Webster house, and most of the town and much of what lay within fifty miles north-by-northwest had been reduced to flaming wreckage. The National Guard was mobilizing, but there was nothing they could do except aid with mass evacuation proceedings; no one could get within two hundred yards of the weapon because of the radiation.

At six-thirty, half a dozen Phantom jets from the Air Force base nearby bombarded it with laser missiles. The missiles failed to destroy it; in fact, it seemed to feed on the heat and released energy, so that its growth rate increased even more rapidly.

In Washington, there was great consternation and panic. The President, his advisers, and the Joint Chiefs of Staff held an emergency meeting to decide whether or not to use an atomic bomb. But by the time they made up their minds it was too late. Much too late.

The thing was then the size of two city blocks, and still growing, and the range of its gigantic muzzle extended beyond the boundaries of the United States—north-by-northwest, toward the Bering Sea and the vast wastes of Russia beyond . . .

THE POOKA

by Peter Tremayne

When Jane and I separated after ten years of marriage it was not an amicable severance. What are those often misquoted lines from Congreve?

> Heav'n has no rage like love to hatred turn'd
> Nor hell a fury like a woman scorn'd.

I have known many people whose marriages have been dissolved and who have gone their differing ways while remaining the best of friends; people who have come to the end of their relationship, mutually recognizing that the ending was inevitable. They have had the foresight to see that it was better to quit while they respected one another, rather than cling to the situation as it deteriorated to a stage where all feeling was destroyed, where the coin flipped from love to hatred.

Regretfully, that was not the way it ended for us.

Jane had been my secretary before our marriage. I was just starting out in a small advertising agency as a junior accountant in those days. Now I am financial director of the same company, which is still a small but prosperous agency.

In fact, it was Jane's second marriage. She had previously been the wife of a young account executive named Garry Pennington, who had worked in our company.

I can recall Garry Pennington well; he was one of those typical brash young men, two years out of university with a second-class degree and on the way to their first million; work hard and play hard. You know the sort. The type you see shrieking down Park Lane in their BMW sports coupé, clad in a Savile Row three-piece suit, on the way to dine at the Hilton Hotel's roof-garden restaurant on an expense account. The only language Pennington understood was how much he could make out of the company for the minimal amount of effort.

Jane was hardly his type. She had joined the company as a secretary. She was not exactly beautiful, more winsome, with a mystical type of attractiveness that caused heads to turn. She had fair skin, freckles, gray eyes and raven-black hair. The type of features which cause you to hear a strumming harp, sea breaking on a granite shoreline, and visualize billowing mists over thrusting mountains. It was no surprise to me to learn that her parents had been Irish and that her first name was really Sineád. She preferred to use the English equivalent of Jane because it saved trouble with insular English attitudes.

Jane and Garry Pennington were like chalk and cheese, but there is a universal rule that like poles repel and unlike poles attract. Within six months of Jane's joining the company, they were married. Young love, perhaps, with all the bewildering pain it entails. They were more or less the same age, about twenty-two. During their courtship, it became a little repugnant to me to see them mooning about the office, holding hands during the coffee breaks and snatching the sly kiss behind an office door. No, I am not prudish. At the time, I was only twenty-four myself. No, the truth of the matter was that I was jealous. I had fallen in love with Jane and I had come to detest Pennington's self-assured, flamboyant attitude.

They had a Catholic wedding—Jane was devoutly Catholic—and the office staff were invited. In fact, only the office staff comprised Jane's guests, for apparently she had no family in England, nor any who made the journey from Ireland to attend. Only Pennington's family attended in force.

I recall that it was not long after they returned from their honeymoon in Ireland that Pennington began to speak slightingly about Jane and once called her "a superstitious bog-Irish gypsy." I was moved to impotent fury on Jane's behalf.

It was only two months after the wedding that it happened.

Garry Pennington was speeding down Park Lane one fine day when his brakes failed and he went straight into the back of an articulated lorry. His death was instantaneous. Jane became a widow.

Old Greyson, our managing director, who was a bit of a sentimentalist, persuaded Jane to stay on with the company and, soon after, when I was promoted, she became my secretary. As the months went by and

Jane began to recover, we started to discover that we had many interests in common. Literature. Theatre. Concerts. We began to go out together now and again and then more frequently. To cut a long story short, eighteen months later, we married. As a widow who had not lost her faith, Jane insisted on a Catholic wedding again. Personally, I am an atheist but, so long as it pleased her, I did not mind.

We spent a three-week honeymoon in Ireland, visiting the Southwest of the country, where, Jane said, her people had come from. She took a great delight in showing me the area, which quelled my misgivings, the spark of jealousy aroused in me because I was following in the footsteps of Garry Pennington. It was an uncharitable thought.

It was while we were on our honeymoon that we acquired our good-luck charm which Jane called "The Pooka." We came to a village called Adrigole, on the Beara Peninsula; it was a small port with a sandy beach. Jane asked me to halt a little way from the village in order that she might show me the vista across Bantry Bay toward the dim, rugged outline of the Sheep's Head Peninsula. I can't think why Jane chose that particular spot, for there were far better scenic parking areas farther along the road. Besides, this spot was near a group of dirty caravans whose occupants, by dress and manners, proclaimed them to be travelers, or "tinkers," as the Irish call them.

We had just left the car and walked to a point to gaze at the gray level of the sea when an old woman came up. She was dirty and had a high, whining voice. She started for me with outstretched hands.

"Ah, lovely sir, may the Lord bless you. Would you not have a coin to spare for luck? I can give you a blessing, sir, a blessing for you . . ."

I shook her beseeching hand roughly away with a muttered exclamation.

"You'll get nothing from me, you old beggar!" I snapped. "Go away or I'll find a policeman."

I have always had an irritation about beggars.

The old woman's voice rose several octaves and she started to shout at me in what I presumed was Irish. Jane afterward told me the words.

"Fágaim mallacht ort! Fuighleacht mallacht ort!"

Her voice halted abruptly and I turned to see Jane placating the crone by handing her some money.

I frowned my disapproval.

"Jane! We can't waste money by giving it away to these sort of people. They are leeches on society. They ought to be made to go out and work, every last one of them."

She turned with a wistful smile.

"Isn't it better to ensure good luck than a curse?"

"Nonsense!" I replied brusquely, climbing into the car. "People have no need to beg in this day and age. They are lazy, idle people."

The old woman fumbled with something in the folds of her shawl and pressed it into Jane's hands.

"*Go raibh maith agat, a cailín ghil mo chroí. An t-ádh an rath! Coinnigh é agus go gcuire sé an t-ádh ort!*"

Then the old woman turned to me and spat on the roadside.

"Keep and cherish her well, my fine *ógánach!* Woe is your lot if you treat her as you treat me!" With that she went scuttling away toward the caravans and disappeared.

"What the hell was that about?" I demanded as Jane climbed into the car. "What was she gabbling about?"

"She was giving me something for luck, that's all," replied Jane.

I chuckled. "Well, I bet the old witch wasn't giving me anything for luck."

Jane's lip drooped. "She cursed you."

"I'll bet! What was it she called me? An ogre?"

"*Ógánach,*" corrected Jane. "It means 'young gentleman,' that's all."

She held a small object in her hands and I stared down at it. It was a small green stone carving. Connemara marble, as I afterward discovered. It was a small, elfin creature, a tiny figurine with a jaunty pointed cap and shoes and a mischievous smile.

"What's that?" I asked.

"It's called a *púca*"; she pronounced it Pooka, and Pooka it became from that time on. "It's a hobgoblin, an imp."

I laughed. "I thought hobgoblins were evil. Well, I'm not superstitious. We'll make it our good-luck charm."

And so "The Pooka" took pride of place on our mantelshelf.

Our marriage started out as a good one. It took me three years before I began to feel dissatisfied. As we grow older and extend the limits of our experience, so we change and develop. Just as we outgrow a suit of clothes, we outgrow our friends and acquaintances. Each man's road in life is marked by the milestones of his discarded likes and dislikes. Wasn't it Saint-Exupéry who said, "To live is to be slowly born"? I suppose I am trying to rationalize my subsequent conduct, because people will find it odd. After all, I had an attractive, loving wife. We hardly ever quarreled. More important, we were great friends, having interests in common. I had a comfortable home and a secure job. So why was I dissatisfied?

To be truthful, I can't quite rationalize that aspect. I needed excitement. The idea of doing something "forbidden" made life less tedious and dull. Yet, why did I need excitement when I had most things that the average man would envy? I can't explain it, except that there is pleasure to be derived from being in a ship being blown about in a storm, an excitement to be derived from the danger. That's why horror movies are so popular. People crave excitement in their lives. Mine came from having casual affairs purely for sexual excitement. Jane had now left the agency and did part-time typing at home, so there was the office romance to offer passing satisfaction, business encounters—models were always hanging around the agency for work. For years my life became that of a "cheat." Oh, I was very careful not to let Jane suspect anything or to hurt her in any way. After all, I would always go back to Jane. She was my wife.

Then I met Elizabeth.

She was tall, blond with a mischievous laugh and a ready sense of fun. She was an executive of a market-research company who were used by our advertising agency. I met her by virtue of mutual business. We had a business lunch one day which was so delightful that I did not get back to the office until 3.45 P.M. It was not the hangdog, "love at first sight" emotion that I had had for Jane, it was a sparkling warmth of feeling which flowed through me when I heard Elizabeth's voice or saw her face.

Two days later, I asked Elizabeth to have a pub lunch with me, pretending that there was a query which I wanted to clear up. She accepted, although, when she arrived at the pub, it was obvious that she had seen through my ruse. To my astonishment, she was not coy or indignant. It was the first of several such assignations. Then came evening rendezvous, and then, well, there were several days when I pretended to Jane that I had to go away on business.

Beth, as I called her, was the complete woman. She was not as intellectual or as mystical as Jane, but Beth's earthy approach was a welcome change. Her sexual appetite was as bold and demanding as mine and she was not afraid to argue when she thought my point of view was wrong. My affair with Beth went on for more than a year. That in itself was unusual and gave me cause to reexamine my lifestyle. Gradually I came to the conclusion that I was in love with Beth; not just "in love," but I "loved" her. She was the perfect partner, because there was no homely, wistful complacency. With her, life was a constant excitement. The excitement was not drawn from the fact that our relationship was illicit; it was drawn from the fact that Beth was an exciting woman. It was as simple as that. Eventually, only one course of action was feasible. I determined to separate from Jane and live with Beth until such time as I secured a divorce and could marry her.

Telling Jane was an experience that I never wish to go through again.

I have heard of people going "berserk" and now I saw it. Gone was the mystic, brooding melancholia which seemed to hang over her most of the time. Instead, her face was filled with a resistless fury, a frenzy of emotions through which she screamed and shouted at me as she had never done before. Her eyes were wide and staring. Some people talk about the Irish temper; I was seeing it for the first time. Finally I shrugged and turned for the door.

"I'll come back for my things when you've calmed down," I said. "Your behavior doesn't alter the fact that I'm leaving."

"I'll never give you a divorce!" she screamed.

"You don't have to," I sneered. "I'm not bound by your Catholicism. If you won't agree to a divorce now, I'll just wait two years and get it myself. You better understand that it is all over between us."

"Curse you!" she shrilled as I slammed the door.

I waited three days before I went back for my bags. To avoid a repeat of the terrible scene, I took John Graham, my solicitor, along. John was a mutual friend as well. Jane let us into the house, demure and self-assured as ever she had been. She was subdued; all sign of her vile temper had gone. John Graham stood nervously by, obviously ill at ease, and declined the drink Jane offered.

"I am sorry that it has to end this way," I said to Jane.

She stared at me; her gaze seemed to be focused behind me, rather than on me.

"I have packed your suitcases with your clothes and personal possessions. If you think there is anything else to which you are entitled, you'd best draw up a list and give it to John to bring round."

I sighed.

"That'll be for the best, I suppose."

She did not appear to have heard me. There was an awkward silence.

"I hope things work out for you, Jane," I said hesitantly.

She stared at me blankly.

John Graham coughed and looked pointedly at me.

"I'll instruct John about the financial arrangements," I pressed. "You won't have to worry."

After another awkward pause, John and I left carrying three large suitcases and a box of my books.

It was a week later that I unpacked the box of books in Beth's bedroom. The transition to life with Beth had not been traumatic. It was a wild, fascinating adventure, totally different to my previous ten years of staid domesticity. Beth had a vast assortment of bohemian friends. We seldom ate in and we were still in the first, excited flush of unbridled love. Then, a week after I moved in, Beth had to go on an overnight business trip for her company, leaving me before the television set with a frozen dinner and her tabby cat to look after. The Friday-evening television programs were terrible, and so I hunted around for a good book. That was when I decided to unpack my books and see if there was something which took my fancy to read.

On top of the books, wrapped in white tissue paper, was the little Connemara-marble figurine—The Pooka, with his elfin hat and coat and mischievous smile.

Frowning, I dialed Jane's telephone number.

She answered immediately, her soft, breathless voice, her familiarity causing me to feel discomfort.

"Jane, I . . . er, I was just unpacking my books and I found The Pooka there." I left the question unspoken.

"You were the one who felt it a symbol of luck," she replied, her voice completely indifferent.

"It was given to you, though," I pointed out.

"It was meant for you," she answered.

There was an awkward pause.

"Are you keeping well?" I felt foolish asking the question.

"Perfectly. John Graham has been round a couple of times to inform me about the financial arrangements."

"Don't hesitate to ask if there is anything—"

"Good-bye," her voice sliced coldly through mine. There came a metallic click as she replaced her receiver.

For a while, I stared at the grinning imp and then, with a sigh, put it on the mantelshelf of the bedroom fireplace. It was a good-luck piece; after all, it had seen me climb from a junior accountant to financial director; had seen me meet Beth, who had brought me more happiness than I had known.

The next morning, dashing to pick Beth up from Heathrow Airport, I cut myself rather badly while shaving, spoiled one of my best shirts and arrived late and cursing at the terminal. But Beth was waiting, waved gaily and came across with a grin.

"My word!" she exclaimed. "You look as if you've been in the wars. Don't say Tabby scratched you?"

I sniffed. "As a matter of fact, your cat and I got along extremely well. We simply ignored each other." I explained ruefully and asked her whether she wanted to go straight home or stop off for a meal.

"Home," she smiled. "I'm tired."

We drove from the airport onto the M4 Motorway, which is the quickest route into London, for Beth's apartment is in Chelsea. I had driven the M4 route more often than I could remember. The motorway was fairly clear of traffic, which was unusual at this time of day. I was cruising at 70 mph in the center lane and coming up to the Chiswick turnoff. Suddenly the wheel was wrenched from my hand, spinning madly.

Beth screamed as the car lurched across the road, cannoned against the center-section crash barrier, and bounced back onto the carriageway, slewing around in a complete circle. I struggled hard with the wheel and, finally, face pouring with cold sweat, brought the vehicle to a halt on the hard shoulder before collapsing over the wheel shaking with fright. I had never been so close to death before.

The next thing I knew was the arrival of a police patrol. The officer was polite and considerate. There had been a bad patch of oil on the center lane, which caused the car to skid. I climbed out of the vehicle and stood with the policeman gazing at the dented offside wing. It would be a panel-beating job as well as a paint-spray job. I shook my head in disgust. Finally, I felt well enough to drive on to the apartment.

Beth, who was nowhere near as shocked as I was, poured us stiff whiskies before we stripped and went under a hot shower together. An hour later in bed the fright of the near accident was dispelled.

"What the hell is that?" demanded Beth suddenly. She sat up in bed and pointed to the mantelshelf.

I squinted and grinned. "That, my love, is The Pooka," I replied.

"The *what?*"

"My good-luck charm. I picked it up in Ireland years ago."

Beth sniffed. "It doesn't look lucky to me. It looks positively fiendish."

I chuckled. "It's brought me good luck."

"You should have had it with you this morning," she replied, reaching for a cigarette.

"We were lucky to come out of that skid alive," I said defensively. "Damned lucky."

"Doubtless thanks to your goblin friend," Beth grimaced before dropping the subject.

The following day was Sunday and we went to a film show before ending up in an exotic Mexican restaurant where I indulged in a large plate of chili con carne. I should not have done so. I awoke in the early hours and only just managed to make it to the bathroom before vomiting.

"Damned restaurant!" muttered Beth as she helped me. "You've got food poisoning."

She went on to say something about five hours passing since the time of the meal and sickness at such a time being indicative of food poisoning. I was past caring. I was wishing for death! It was pure misery. But, at last, I was able to fall asleep. In the morning I awoke sore and exhausted but feeling better. Beth telephoned my office and explained that I was going to spend the day in bed. She also reported the restaurant to the health authorities.

That evening, I was feeling much better. Beth prepared a fairly simple meal and then started to call her cat for its plate of food. The cat was usually on the balcony of the apartment. It was not an adventurous animal and hardly ever stirred from the place. That evening, it was nowhere to be found.

Beth turned to me with a frown: "Have you seen Tabby?" she asked.

I confessed that I had been too busy wrapped in my own misery to notice the activities of her feline friend.

We ate our meal, watched some television and while I went for a shower, Beth called the cat again, with no better response than before.

"Where ever can it be?" she frowned as she came to bed.

"Even a cat has to go on the tiles once in a while," I murmured sleepily.

She dug me sharply with her elbow. "He's been doctored, idiot!"

"Then, he's probably developed into a peeping tom," I quipped, ducking as she went to hit me with her pillow.

We thought no more of the animal until the next morning. The caretaker of the building rang the bell with a morose face, and a cardboard box tucked under one arm.

"Excuse me, miss," he said as Beth opened the door, "would this be your animal . . . ?" He removed the lid from the cardboard box and held it out. The caretaker was clearly no animal lover, or respectful of the feelings of anyone who was.

Beth's cat lay squashed and bloody in the box.

"Found it outside the front door. Seems to me like it was run over by a car."

Beth was upset. She had kept the animal for four years and grown quite attached to it; you know how some people can be about cats. I can take them or leave them; independent, willful creatures.

Although the cat's death had upset her, Beth decided to go in to work to take her mind off the matter. I was restless. I telephoned old Greyson, my managing director, and told him I still felt queasy. He sounded preoccupied, and while he told me to take the day off, he seemed anxious that I return to the office as soon as possible.

I wandered about the apartment for a while and then decided to give Beth a surprise. I took out the vacuum cleaner, duster and brush and began to give the place a thorough clean. I was dusting the mantelshelf in the bedroom—lifting the objects to dust—when I found myself picking up The Pooka. The little green imp was grinning away.

I stared hard at it.

There was a strange hint of malevolency on its features which I could swear I had never seen before. Mischief—yes; but the grin was more pronounced than I had previously observed. I wondered why I had ever doubted the expression on the face of the creature; it was positively malignant, its tiny features were filled with maliciousness and animosity.

"Come on," I muttered, replacing it. "You're supposed to bring me luck, remember?"

I turned. I know it sounds foolish, but as I turned I tripped over the lead of the vacuum cleaner and went sprawling across the floor, banging my head against the leg of a chair.

As I ruefully picked myself up, I caught sight of the figurine. Was it my imagination or was the damned thing grinning more broadly than it had been before?

Nonsense! I cursed myself for a fool. Ten years with Jane was making me believe that an inanimate object was capable of feeling. Jane, for all her intellectual qualities, still had that superstitious quality that is common to the Celts.

Well, the days passed and it seemed that our run of bad luck was over. Well, of course, I never really believed in bad luck, but it is strange, isn't it, how bad things never happen in single events?

Well, life resumed its normal state. I returned to the agency to find that Greyson was worried about a "cash-flow" problem, as he called it. He wanted me to devote myself to gathering all unpaid accounts. Beth and I began to go out and visit friends, mainly Beth's friends. Unlike Jane, Beth had numerous acquaintances in the artistic world. Her circle was far more cosmopolitan than the one in which I had previously mixed. One evening, we went to a party held by some artist and one of the guests was a clairvoyant who went by the grandiose title of Count Elhanan Roscovski. The count was supposed to be famous; not that I would know, because I always regarded clairvoyants as charlatans, peddlers of gobbledegook. When I was introduced to Count Roscovski I held out my hand with an expression of amused cynicism.

As he touched my hand, a strange thing happened. He jerked as if he had touched a live electric wire. His bright black eyes stared wildly into mine. His lips moved slowly.

"An rud do scríobhann an púca leigheann sé féin é!"

At first I thought he was speaking in some Slavonic language, but I suddenly picked out the word *púca* and frowned.

"What did you say?" I demanded, as the other guests crowded round in interest.

The count just stood rigidly before me, eyes staring into mine.

"An rud do scríobhann an púca leigheann sé féin é!"

I frowned at him suspiciously.

"Is that Irish that you are speaking? What does it mean?"

It was as if he had not heard me at all.

I turned to Beth and whispered: "Beth, just write down the words—put down the phonetics if you can. This character has obviously gone into his act but I'm curious."

Beth fumbled with her bag, sought an address book and pencil just as Roscovski said the sentence for a third time. Then he added:

"Chughat an púca!"

His eyes closed and he staggered forward as if he would pitch upon his face. Several hands caught the man and he looked around him, bewildered.

"I feel unwell," he said, a trifle plaintively. "I must go home."

Our host was genial. "What were you saying to this gentleman, Count? You were speaking in a strange tongue."

Roscovski gazed at me perplexed and a little flustered. "I do not know. I do not remember."

"Oh, come on!" I cried. "You don't know what you said a moment ago?"

Roscovski shrugged. "I don't feel well. I must have had a . . . a sensation. I must go home."

He made to turn, hesitated and glanced at me. "I feel danger for you, sir," he suddenly whispered. "Great danger."

Then he was gone, leaving behind the guests chuckling in amusement at the party piece and congratulating the host and myself on a fine piece of theater.

Beth came to my side with a frown and handed me a slip of paper.

"I think I managed to get down the phonetics of what he said," she sighed. "I've no idea what language it's in. It might be gibberish, for all I know."

I drew her aside, away from the curious revelers.

"I've an idea that it is Irish," I said, a strange, cold fear lurking in my mind—a fear I could not articulate.

"What makes you say that?" She was curious.

I told her about the single word *púca*, which I recognized.

She smiled and shook her head. Beth had a B.A. in English.

"The word occurs in Anglo-Saxon and means goblin there as well. It is where we get the modern English Puck or Pouke. You must have read Kipling's *Puck of Pook's Hill* when you were a kid?"

"I thought it was Irish." I frowned.

"So it is. But it also occurs in Welsh as *pwca* and Cornish as *bucca*. You see, all those languages borrowed it from the Old Norse *púki.*"

I stared at her in astonishment.

She chuckled. "I'm not really that academic. My thesis was on early Norse loan words in English. I know nothing else, but give me a Norse loan word and I'll bore the pants off you."

"All the same," I grinned back, "I believe it's Irish. I've a friend who has a contact at the Irish Embassy. He might be able to translate."

The next morning, at my office, I telephoned my friend and he told me that he would see what he could do. Then all thought of the incident was chased from my mind. Old man Greyson rang on my internal telephone and asked to see me. His voice was off, strangely subdued. Frowning, I hurried to his office.

"I'll get right down to it," he said as I entered and shut the door. "The company is about to go bust."

My jaw dropped. "Is this a joke?"

He shook his head sadly. "Not a bit of it. You'll recall that we've been pursuing the policy of the one big client?"

Indeed. In fact, it was my idea. Our advertising agency was a small one, with only a limited number of resources. It had been my plan to instigate a policy of consolidation by closing down our smaller accounts and relying on one big account which we could back with the entire staff at our disposal.

Greyson now thrust a copy of the *Financial Times* at me.

The company in which we had placed all our faith, a large frozen-food manufacturer, had announced that it was going into liquidation. An official receiver had been appointed.

I frowned. "But we must have assets to tide us over until we obtain new clients?"

Greyson shrugged. "We put all the financial assets we had into the last campaign for the company. They owe us a hundred thousand pounds. We've barely enough in the bank to pay everyone a week's wages in lieu of notice."

"We must be able to raise a loan?" I countered desperately.

"I've been trying. Advertising agencies are two-a-penny. We have no collateral."

"I'll think of something," I replied grimly, trotting back to my office.

Of all the bad luck! How could something like this happen? The agency had been doing so well.

At lunchtime I was due to meet Beth at the reception of the office block. She was late; in fact, she didn't show at all. I telephoned her office on her direct number but there was no reply.

It was late in the afternoon when my telephone rang.

An impersonal voice asked: "Do you know a Miss Elizabeth Atkins, sir?"

That cold, uneasy feeling started to creep over my limbs.

"I know Beth. Is anything the matter?"

The voice sounded suddenly troubled. "Did you know her well, sir?"

"Who the hell is this?" I demanded suddenly, fear making me angry.

"This is Rochester Row Police Station, sir. I'm afraid that there has been a traffic accident."

The coldness was unbearable.

"Beth . . . ?"

"Miss Atkins was involved in an incident with a motorcycle at—"

"For God's sake!" I nearly screamed. "How is Beth?"

"I'm afraid Miss Atkins died shortly after her admittance to Charing Cross Hospital. We found your name and telephone number in her address book and are trying to trace the next of kin. Were you a close friend, sir?"

"I was her bloody lover!" I snarled as I slammed down the receiver.

God knows how I fought my way out of the office back to the apartment, where a policeman confronted me. I was aware of sad, sympathetic utterances, mumbled words of condolence, of commiseration, of consolation. I was aware of people drifting to and fro like shadows and then . . . suddenly I was alone in the bedroom of Beth's apartment with the telephone jangling persistently beside me.

I reached out automatically.

It was a strange, lilting Irish voice. The man introduced himself as the acquaintance of my friend.

"This lot of nonsense you transcribed into phonetics," chuckled the voice, "now where would you have picked up such stuff?"

I tried hard to concentrate. "What do you mean?"

"Jesus!" exclaimed the man. *"Chughat an púca!* Beware of The Pooka, indeed! A pooka is—"

"I know what a pooka is!" I exclaimed. "What else does it mean?"

" 'Tis only an old proverb: what a pooka writes, he deciphers himself."

The fear, the awesome dread, turned into mindless panic, causing me to slam down the receiver. My eyes turned unwillingly to the little green marble figure on the mantelshelf. There it was, grinning down at me, its grin wider, more malevolent than ever.

With a cry of rage, I made a grab at it, thinking to throw it into the fireplace, to smash it into a thousand fragments. As I swept my hand upward, I felt a terrible electric shock, which threw me back against the wall.

I lay staring at the figurine in wide-eyed perturbation. My heart was palpitating with apprehension.

Beware of The Pooka!

This was no symbol of good luck! No charm for fortuity and prosperity. It was a symbol of my damnation!

Thoughts tumbled in my mind.

Jane! I had to see Jane! She would know what it meant, what to do. She would be able to help me out of this terrifying nightmare into which I had drifted. I crawled unsteadily to my feet and stumbled from the apartment.

It was twilight and raining by the time I arrived at our house—Jane's house—in the suburbs. I turned up the drive and pressed the bell savagely. There was no answer, but a light was burning in the hall. I pressed the bell again, letting it peal long and loudly. Then I heard a noise. Jane's figure appeared behind the frosted-glass panel of the door, fumbling with the locks.

She swung the door open and stood there, gazing in surprise. Her hair was tousled and she wore only a scanty dressing gown.

"What do you want?" She frowned belligerently, having recovered from her astonishment.

"The Pooka!" I gasped. I could feel my face working in my anxiety. "Jane, The Pooka! It has a curse on it."

She stared at me for a moment before her face creased into a smile. "You don't believe in curses, surely?" she chuckled cynically.

"For God's sake, Jane! I'm serious! So many terrible things have been happening to me—Beth's dead! My company's gone bust and there are countless other things which have happened. It's a curse! I

swear it, Jane! I swear it! You must know . . . you must take it back.
. . ." I stood sobbing like a child.

"Take it back?" came Jane's sneer. "Why should I do that?"

I stared at her wild-eyed. "There was never bad luck with you. You
can negate whatever curse it holds. You must take it back."

"Must I?"

It was then I caught a movement on the stair and glanced behind
her.

John Graham stood hesitantly there, a trifle self-conscious. He was
naked except for a bath towel folded around his middle. "Are you all
right, darling?" he asked.

Jane gazed at me with a triumphant smile before turning. "Yes,
John. He's just leaving." She turned back to me, her eyes suddenly
filled with hate.

"Jane!" I cried in desperation. "For pity's sake!"

"Ah, pity and charity is something you know much about," she
whispered softly.

"I don't understand. For God's sake, Jane, tell me what is happening
to me. Why is it happening?"

"Every why has a wherefore." She made to shut the door and then
hesitated and stared coldly at me. "Take away the cause and the effect
ceases. I trusted you and you took my trust and trampled it. I gave you
my heart and you took it in your hands and crushed it. My love for you
was not the love of a dog for the sheep, it was the love of a salmon for
the river. You have hurt me beyond measure. Now you must pay.
Should I care now if you are pricked by the thorns which you planted?"

The door slammed in my face.

I heard her merry laugh mingling with the deep tones of John
Graham's chuckle.

Shocked and numbed, I staggered away from the house, my mind in
a turmoil. As I came out of the gate into the night-black street, head
involuntarily down against the sheeting rain, a dark figure stirred by the
black bushes. It was the figure of a bent old woman.

"Bless you, sir. Can you spare a coin for an old woman, a coin for the
sake of luck?"

The accent was familiar.

Habits of a lifetime take a long while to die. I turned away with a
curse. My own state of mind made the violence of my reactions

stronger. "Go and pollute your own country! How dare you bother people in a public street!"

The old woman chuckled. "No, you have not changed much, my fine *duine uasal*—my fine gentleman."

There was something in the voice, something about her which conjured up a vague memory.

I turned and frowned toward the black-shawled creature. "Do I know you?"

"Right enough, sir."

She moved forward slightly and her wizened features were briefly illuminated by the streetlamp.

"You!" I cried. "You were the one who gave us The Pooka! You caused the curse!"

"Not I," chuckled the old woman. "You caused your own bad luck, your own cursing. The Pooka was given to your wife. When you hurt her, that hurt rebounded on you. There is always a cause and effect."

I stared at her aghast, not wanting to believe what I was hearing and yet believing.

"I saw your character on your face ten years ago, when you treated me discourteously at Adrigole. I knew that someday you would hurt your wife. It was the same with her first husband."

"Her first husband?" I was totally bemused now. What did this crone know of Jane's first husband?

"She brought him to see me," she went on as if reading my thoughts. "He was the perfect gentleman. The suave English *duine uasal*. He treated me well, and she"—the old woman jerked her head toward my house—Jane's house—"she thought that me being a tinker would not matter to him. So she told him. I knew he wouldn't want her when he realized the truth. I gave her a pooka for protection."

There was a clawing in my stomach as I tried to fathom out the meaning of what she was saying. "Are you talking about Garry Pennington?"

"That was his name," she assented.

"Pennington was killed in a car crash—" I began but was interrupted by her chuckle.

"So he was! So he was!"

"What are you telling me? The Pooka was responsible?"

"Oh no, no. *He* was responsible. Man is responsible for all his actions. He rejected her and hurt her."

"Rejected Jane? Hurt Jane?"

"Jane . . . Sineád . . . whatever you call her in this country."

I tried to gather my thoughts and make a final attempt to understand. "Sineád? How do you know Jane's real name? Why should Pennington have rejected Jane because she introduced him to you? How do you know Jane?"

The old woman's laughing was uncontrollable. "A fine mother I'd be if I didn't know my own daughter."

I staggered back a pace, fear clawing with icy hands at my heart.

Jane's mother! Now it made sense. And at that moment I knew that there would be no appeal. I read the cold glaze of hatred in the old woman's eyes just as surely as I had read the hatred in Jane's face. The sentence for my misdeeds had been passed. My fate was inevitable.

I tried to bring my gaze back to the old woman, but she had gone into the blackness and driving rain of the evening.

There was nothing for it, nothing left but to return to Beth's apartment, back to the grinning imp-like figurine, back to The Pooka. Was it an instrument of retribution or justice?

THE MAN WHO LOVED WATER

by Craig Shaw Gardner

He had always loved the water. A clear lake like this, fed by mountain streams, was his idea of heaven.

When they sat out on the dock on hot, sun-filled afternoons, they could see every stone on the bottom, as if they were looking through glass. They sat on dock's edge and dangled their feet in the cool water. Silver minnows glinted in the sun as they darted just above the stones.

He looked up to see Anna, laughing behind her sunglasses at one of Peter's jokes. She was very beautiful, sitting there just then, with her blue bikini and summer tan just the way she liked it. Her blond hair shone brilliantly in the sun. Even her piña colada seemed to glow.

He smiled at his wife, and Anna smiled back. We have moments like this, he thought, every now and then. He was a very happy man.

"I think I'll go in for a swim," he announced.

"Sounds like a good idea, dear." Anna sipped her piña colada. "And I think I'll sit here and watch you from the dock. Do you want to go in, Peter?"

"No." Peter scratched at his beard and shook his dark brown curls. "I just finished my second beer. Best that I stay out for a bit. If you get in any trouble, Dave, just whistle. We'll be watching you from here."

Dave walked out to the end of the dock and dove.

To sit on the dock by the lake may have been a perfect world, but when he dove beneath the surface he entered another world altogether. Dave always opened his eyes right away. Ever since he was a little kid, this had been his place, his peaceful retreat from the world. The water itself looked grey-green in the distance, and it filtered the light from above in a special way. It made the colors of stones and plants jump out at you, much the way the sun would illuminate the fallen leaves on an autumn evening, colors too bright to be real, shining for an instant, then gone with the dark.

But the colors were here, underwater, all day long. Dave propelled himself farther out into the lake with a couple of good breaststrokes, then swam to the surface for air. He was already a good distance from the dock. He waved at the tiny figures of Anna and Peter. Peter saw him and waved back.

He dove under the water again. It was cool against his skin. He felt almost weightless. He swam to the bottom, a good twelve feet down here, and startled a small trout hiding in the weeds.

He'd loved this since he was a kid, spent every minute he could in the lake, whole summers in the water. He remembered how his mother used to try to get him to come out for lunch. "David! Get out here this minute or your soup will get cold!" She always got angry with him for a moment before she gave up. Finally, she'd call: "You've got to come out sometime!" and climb the path back to the cottage. When Dave heard her say that, he knew he was free. He always did come out, but not until he was good and ready.

The lake did odd things with light, and it did much the same with sound. It muffled some noises, and made others seem much closer than they actually were. Maybe it had something to do with the currents; he wasn't sure. Dave heard a motorboat, far away. And as he swam back beneath the surface, he could hear Peter and Anna.

"—we have to tell him."

"How can we? Anna—"

The voices faded for an instant, then returned.

"—can't be ready."

"You're underestimating Dave. You always did—"

Then the voices were gone, carried away by the waves.

Dave felt a pressure in his chest. Something was wrong. It sounded like an argument of some sort. Dave didn't like arguments. He felt very cold in the icy lake water, and, at the same time, he felt a little guilty, as if he had eavesdropped on a private conversation. They were his friends. Sometimes Anna got a little overprotective. He was sure they'd tell him their problems soon enough. And he'd act surprised, as if he had never heard the comments carried by the water. He kicked to the surface and noisily swam the last dozen or so feet to the dock.

Anna had finished her drink. The empty glass rested by her thigh.

"Enjoy your swim?" Peter called.

"I wish you wouldn't go quite so far out, honey," Anna chided. "What would we do if something happened to you?"

"Don't worry so much about me." Dave stood on the dock and dried himself off with a towel. "I'd spend my life in that lake if I could. What say we go upstairs and get another drink?"

He snapped the towel in Anna's direction. She frowned at him in mock anger, another of the little games they played. She used to yell at him a lot more when he would disappear into deep water; something about it really frightened her. She still mentioned it when he went out too far, but not like before. The old fighting spirit was gone. It was like she was supposed to say it, so she said it. In a way, it was like another game. Parts of their marriage had gotten like that.

Oh, well. Dave supposed that meant their marriage was settling down. You couldn't act like newlyweds forever.

Dave followed the other two up the hill. Actually, he was glad Peter could come down for a few days. The three of them always got on well together, and having a third person around kept Anna and him from getting into their little disagreements.

Dave sighed. He supposed that he and Anna should sit down sometime and figure out just what they were fighting about. But it wasn't that bad. And besides, this was vacation.

"Why so glum, chum?" Peter patted him on the back. Peter, on occasion, had a special gift for triteness. Dave still managed a smile.

"Lost in my own little world." Dave forced a laugh. "It's the lake. I've been coming down here since I was a kid. It makes me introspective."

"Hey, this is your vacation. Have a drink and relax. I think there's a ball game on."

Anna led the way into the cottage. She'd get dinner ready. Peter insisted on making the drinks. Dave found himself in the living room with time on his hands. He wandered over to the picture window that looked out across the water. It was late afternoon now, and the sun had begun its arc toward the high hills above the far shore. Dave always liked the way sunlight lit the waves at this time of day. Golden ripples washed over the lake's surface.

Peter wandered in and turned on the TV. The Yankees were losing. Dave found a drink in his hand. He took a sip. It was a Tom Collins. A moment later, they ate their dinner, and talked about things other than water.

It wasn't until afterward, sitting and drinking coffee, that the conversation got interesting.

"It *is* half a mile deep," Dave insisted.

"You're full of it," Peter replied.

"No, the lake was formed by glaciers in the ice age. And those glaciers dug real deep."

Anna patted Peter's shoulder. "He's right, Peter. Glaciers dug up this whole area."

"Really?" Peter shrugged. "Well, if Anna says so, I guess I'm convinced."

"Some parts of the lake have never been explored," Dave continued. "Just too deep. Which, of course, leads us to the subject of the Monster of the Lakes."

Coffee spewed from Peter's mouth. He made a sound halfway between a laugh and a choke.

"Oh, God," he gasped. "Not while I'm drinking. You're crazy, Dave."

"David," Anna chided. "Do we have to go into that again?"

"Anna's jaded. She's heard it all before." Dave winked at Peter. His friend raised his eyebrows in mock surprise.

But Dave knew it was more than that. Anna had always been a little afraid of the water. In their first summer here together, she'd overcome her fear, or so it seemed, and swum in the lake with Dave. But each succeeding summer, she swam less and less, and now she didn't go into the lake at all. She seemed content to just sit on the dock and watch.

When the two of them were first together, one night, very late, just for fun, Dave had told her about the monster. It was a Loch Ness sort of thing, your basic, garden-variety sea serpent. Well, lake serpent, at least. It was, of course, kept alive by Indian magic. There had been Indians here once, of course. Still was a reservation around here somewhere. Well, he had described all the rumors in great detail, elaborating here and there where he felt it was appropriate. Anna had loved it. Their relationship was still a little tentative then. She had needed an excuse to hold him. Dave had been happy to use the monster for such positive purpose.

Anna was getting upset as Dave wove his story now, even more elaborate with the passing years. Peter roared with laughter. He didn't see the small lines form at the edges of Anna's mouth and eyes.

"David! Stop all this! You are no longer amusing!"

Peter tried, unsuccessfully, to stop laughing. Somehow, David couldn't let the whole thing die. Not yet.

"And then, the horrible thing, glistening scales and all, rises from the mire at lake bottom." He spread his arms wide and roared.

"Roooharrr!"

Teeth bared, he lunged for Anna.

She slapped him across the face.

He stared at his wife. He didn't feel like being funny anymore. He realized there was anger beneath his horseplay. He didn't feel it anymore, but he recognized its absence. Now, all he felt was empty.

Peter's voice finally broke the silence. "Hey, guys. Let's keep it cool, huh?"

Dave's anger came flooding back. All it had needed was a focus. Peter fit the role nicely.

"Would you stay out of this, Peter? I don't know why you're here, anyways. Anna and I can never have a moment alone together!"

"David!" Anna scolded. "Don't be such a child. It's just like you to blame Peter for all your own problems!"

Dave looked at his wife as if he had been slapped again. How could she say that? She didn't understand him at all!

He found himself getting really angry now. He turned away from the other two and walked out of the cottage.

He stopped walking when he reached the beach. Small stones crunched beneath his feet, setting up a counterpoint to the katydids in the trees. He kicked a rock out into the lake. Down here, he didn't feel quite as angry anymore. It was hard to be upset when he stood by the edge of the water.

Anna called his name from the cottage. Dave felt the anger stir inside him again. He looked up at the night sky. There was no moon tonight, nothing to shine off the lake at all, but a thousand stars washed across the sky. He decided to go for a swim.

He stripped off his shirt and pants and walked to the end of the dock and dove. The water covered him, a welcome blanket of darkness. No light reached below the surface. He was alone with his thoughts.

He concentrated on pulling himself through the water, the breaststroke beneath, the crawl when he reached the surface for air, then down below again. The pull of his muscles against the lake was reassuring, something solid his mind could feel. He would push the anger out, swim until all emotion was gone.

Why was he so afraid of his anger?

Maybe he was afraid he would lose Anna. But what, just now, did Anna and he really have? Why did he taunt her that way?

Somehow, in his anger, he felt he was the monster of the lake.

He imagined Anna, still calling him. Maybe she was down on the beach, looking for him. Peter would be calling him too. Dave wouldn't have gone swimming, all alone, on a night as dark as this. Why doesn't he come out when we call?

Dave felt a moment's glee at the thought of upsetting the others. But that wasn't very mature, was it? The emotion was childish in its intensity. Maybe Anna was right about him after all.

It was the flip side of all those afternoons, refusing to obey his mother. All this swimming was just an escape. He had to grow up and obey himself. He had to come out of the water sometime.

He swam back to shore.

There was no one on the beach. Anna and Peter must still be up in the cottage.

He found them on the living room floor without any clothes on.

He roared like the monster of the lake. Anna pulled away from Peter's embrace. She looked at Dave and screamed. Peter was saying something to Dave. His voice was reasonable, assured. Somehow, Dave couldn't make out the words. He looked right at the two of them on the floor, but he could no longer see them. Something was playing tricks with the sound, tricks with the light.

Somehow, Dave found himself in the kitchen. Somehow, Dave found his right hand around a carving knife.

Peter was in the kitchen too. "Dave, stop it." Peter's voice was very far away. Dave looked dumbly, down at the knife in his hand. Peter grabbed Dave's arm. Dave saw Anna, watching them both from the doorway to the living room. His hand jerked spasmodically.

Dave felt pain below his rib cage, as if his anger had burned through his stomach. He looked down to see the knife protruding from his waist, blood pouring from a long tear in his flesh. Something inside wanted to come out. He fell onto the kitchen floor.

He could no longer see, but he could hear their voices.

"Dave?"

"I think he's dead."

"Peter!"

"You saw what happened. He had a knife. He was crazy. He'd been crazy a long time. You know that."

"I'm so sorry, Dave. Peter and I—you would never understand—we've loved each other for a long time—I never wanted this—" Anna began to cry.

"It's no use crying for the dead."

The voices were growing fainter. Dave strained to hear.

"What are we going to do with him?"

"Should we call the police?"

"They'd never understand. I have to stay with you."

"Oh, Peter—"

Dave couldn't hear any more.

It was cool where Dave was. Cool and quiet and dark. Dave opened his eyes.

He was back in the water. It was still night, or he was very, very deep, where light never penetrated. Still, Dave wasn't afraid. He loved the water.

Far away, he heard Peter and Anna. Sometimes they talked, and sometimes they made love.

They would be happy together. Anna would get over her grief.

Dave tried his muscles. They were stiff at first. He had to remember how to do the breaststroke.

Dave had been crazy. No one could talk to him any more. It was better for all of them this way.

Dave kicked his feet, propelling himself underwater, moving closer to the shore.

Such a shame about Dave. The search parties hadn't found a thing, just as they'd suspected. But the lake was so deep. It was so foolish to swim alone at night.

Dave's strokes were sure now, so much more powerful than they had ever been before.

Anna and Peter told each other, over and over again, that everything would be all right. They knew they could take comfort, alone, in each other's arms.

Dave could sense the shore rising beneath him. He was under something now, wooden boards, a dock. Two people stood above him.

He had to come out of the water sometime.

BLOOD GOTHIC

by Nancy Jones Holder

She wanted to have a vampire lover. She wanted it so badly that she kept waiting for it to happen. One night, soon, she would awaken to wings flapping against the window and then take to wearing velvet ribbons and cameo lockets around her delicate, pale neck. She knew it.

She immersed herself in the world of her vampire lover: She devoured gothic romances, consumed late-night horror movies. Visions of satin capes and eyes of fire shielded her from the harshness of the daylight, from mortality and the vain and meaningless struggles of the world of the sun. Days as a kindergarten teacher and evenings with some overly eager, casual acquaintance could not pull her from her secret existence: always a ticking portion of her brain planned, proceeded, waited.

She spent her meager earnings on dark antiques and intricate clothes. Her wardrobe was crammed with white negligees and ruffled underthings. No crosses and no mirrors, particularly not in her bedroom. White tapered candles stood in pewter sconces, and she would read late into the nights by their smoky flickerings, she scented and ruffled, hair combed loosely about her shoulders. She glanced at the window often.

She resented lovers—though she took them, thrilling to the fullness of life in them, the blood and the life—who insisted upon staying all night, burning their breakfast toast and making bitter coffee. Her kitchen, of course, held nothing but fresh ingredients and copper and ironware; to her chagrin, she could not do without ovens or stoves or refrigerators. Alone, she carried candles and bathed in cool water.

She waited, prepared. And at long last, her vampire lover began to come to her in dreams. They floated across the moors, glided through the fields of heather. He carried her to his crumbling castle, undressing her, pulling off her diaphanous gown, caressing her lovely body, until, in the height of passion, he bit into her arched neck, drawing the life out of her and replacing it with eternal damnation and eternal love.

She awoke from these dreams drenched in sweat and feeling exhausted. The kindergarten children would find her unusually quiet and self-absorbed, and it frightened her when she rubbed her spotless neck and smiled wistfully. *Soon and soon and soon,* her veins chanted, in prayer and anticipation. *Soon.*

The children were her only regret. She would not miss her inquisitive relatives and friends, the ones who frowned and studied her as if she were a portrait of someone they knew they were supposed to recognize. Those, who urged her to drop by for an hour, to come with them to films, to accompany them to the seashore. Those, who were connected to her—or thought they were—by the mere gesturing of the long and milky hands of Fate. Who sought to distract her from her one true passion; who sought to discover the secret of that passion. For, true to the sacredness of her vigil for her vampire lover, she had never spoken of him to a single earthly, earthbound soul. It would be beyond them, she knew. They would not comprehend a bond of such intentioned sacrifice.

But she would regret the children. Never would a child of their love coo and murmur in the darkness; never would his proud and noble features soften at the sight of the mother and her child of his loins. It was her single sorrow.

Her vacation was coming. June hovered like the mist and the children squirmed in anticipation. Their own true lives would begin in June. She empathized with the shining eyes and smiling faces, knowing their wait was as agonizing as her own. Silently, as the days closed in, she bade each of them a tender farewell, holding them as they threw their little arms around her neck and pressed fervent summertime kisses on her cheeks.

She booked her passage to London on a ship. Then to Romania, Bulgaria, Transylvania. The hereditary seat of her beloved; the fierce, violent backdrop of her dreams. Her suitcases opened themselves to her long, full skirts and her brooches and lockets. She peered into her hand mirror as she packed it. "I am getting pale," she thought, and the idea both terrified and delighted her.

She became paler, thinner, more exhausted as her trip wore on. After recovering from the disappointment of the raucous, modern cruise ship, she raced across the Continent to find refuge in the creaky trains and taverns she had so yearned for. Her heart thrilled as she meandered past the black silhouettes of ruined fortresses and ancient manor houses. She sat for hours in the mists, praying for the howling wolf to find her, for the bat to come and join her.

She took to drinking wine in bed, deep, rich, blood-red burgundy that glowed in the candlelight. She melted into the landscape within days, and cringed as if from the crucifix itself when flickers of her past life, her American, false existence, invaded her serenity. She did not keep a diary; she did not count the days as her summer slipped away from her. She only rejoiced that she grew weaker.

It was when she was counting out the coins for a Gypsy shawl that she realized she had no time left. Tomorrow she must make for Frankfurt and from there fly back to New York. The shopkeeper nudged her, inquiring if she were ill, and she left with her treasure, trembling. She began to cry, of course.

She flung herself on her own rented bed. "This will not do. This will not do." She pleaded with the darkness. "You must come for me tonight. I have done everything for you, my beloved, loved you above all else. You must save me." She sobbed until she ached.

She skipped her last meal of veal and paprika and sat quietly in her room. The innkeeper brought her yet another bottle of burgundy and after she assured him that she was quite all right, just a little tired, he wished his guest a pleasant trip home.

The night wore on; though her book was open before her, her eyes were riveted to the windows, her hands clenched around the wineglass as she sipped steadily, like a creature feeding. Oh, to feel him against her veins, emptying her and filling her!

Soon and soon and soon . . .

Then, all at once, it happened. The windows rattled, flapped inward. A great shadow, a curtain of ebony, fell across the bed, and the room began to whirl, faster, faster still; and she was consumed with a bitter, deathly chill. She heard, rather than saw, the wineglass crash to the floor, and struggled to keep her eyes open as she was overwhelmed, engulfed, taken.

"Is it you?" she managed to whisper through teeth that rattled with delight and cold and terror. "Is it finally to be?"

Freezing hands touched her everywhere: her face, her breasts, the desperate offering of her arched neck. Frozen and strong and never-dying. Sinking, she smiled in a rictus of mortal dread and exultation. Eternal damnation, eternal love. Her vampire lover had come for her at last.

When her eyes opened again, she let out a howl and shrank against the searing brilliance of the sun. Hastily, they closed the curtains and quickly told her where she was: home again, where everything was warm and pleasant and she was safe from the disease that had nearly killed her.

She had been ill before she had left the States. By the time she had reached Transylvania, her anemia had been acute. Had she never noticed her own pallor, her lassitude?

Anemia. Her smile was a secret on her white lips. So they thought, but he *had* come for her, again and again. In her dreams. And on that night, he had meant to take her finally to his castle forever, to crown her the best-beloved one, his love of the moors and mists.

She had but to wait, and he would finish the deed.

Soon and soon and soon.

She let them fret over her, wrapping her in blankets in the last days of summer. She endured the forced cheer of her relatives, allowed them to feed her rich food and drink in hopes of restoring her.

But her stomach could no longer hold the nourishment of their kind; they wrung their hands and talked of stronger measures when it became clear that she was wasting away.

At the urging of the doctor, she took walks. Small ones at first, on painfully thin feet. Swathed in wool, cowering behind sunglasses, she took tiny steps like an old woman. As she moved through the summer hours, her neck burned with an ungovernable pain that would not cease until she rested in the shadows. Her stomach lurched at the sight of grocery-store windows. But at the butcher's, she paused, and licked her lips at the sight of the raw, bloody meat.

But she did not go to him. She grew neither worse nor better.

"I am trapped," she whispered to the night as she stared into the flames of a candle by her bed. "I am disappearing between your world and mine, my beloved. Help me. Come for me." She rubbed her neck, which ached and throbbed but showed no outward signs of his devotion. Her throat was parched, bone-dry, but water did not quench her thirst.

At long last, she dreamed again. Her vampire lover came for her as before, joyous in their reunion. They soared above the crooked trees at the foothills, streamed like black banners above the mountain crags to his castle. He could not touch her enough, worship her enough, and they were wild in their abandon as he carried her in her diaphanous gown to the gates of his fortress.

But at the entrance, he shook his head with sorrow and could not let her pass into the black realm with him. His fiery tears seared her neck, and she thrilled to the touch of the mark even as she cried out for him as he left her, fading into the vapors with a look of entreaty in his dark, flashing eyes.

Something was missing; he required a boon of her before he could bind her against his heart. A thing that she must give to him . . .

She walked in the sunlight, enfeebled, cowering. She thirsted, hungered, yearned. Still she dreamed of him, and still he could not take the last of her unto himself.

Days and nights and days. Her steps took her finally to the schoolyard, where once, only months before, she had embraced and kissed the children, thinking never to see them again. They were all there, who had kissed her cheeks so eagerly. Their silvery laughter was like the tinkling of bells as dust motes from their games and antics whirled around their feet. How free they seemed to her who was so troubled, how content and at peace.

The children.

She shambled forward, eyes widening behind the shields of smoky glass.

He required something of her first.

Her one regret. Her only sorrow.

She thirsted. The burns on her neck pulsated with pain.

Tears of gratitude welled in her eyes for the revelation that had not come too late. Weeping, she pushed open the gate of the schoolyard and reached out a skeleton-limb to a child standing apart from the rest, engrossed in a solitary game of cat's cradle. Tawny-headed, ruddy-cheeked, filled with the blood and the life.

For him, as a token of their love.

"My little one, do you remember me?" she said softly.

The boy turned. And smiled back uncertainly in innocence and trust.

Then, as she came for him, swooped down on him like a great, winged thing, with eyes that burned through the glasses, teeth that flashed once, twice . . .

soon and soon and soon.

SAND

by Alan Ryan

"Dave," Patty said as they made their way through the crowded parking lot, "there's a man in that car with red sand coming out of his ears."

Dave was walking ahead of her, his arms loaded with packages, most of them containing boxes of Christmas decorations and fragile ornaments. A bright red plastic shopping bag swung clumsily from his left wrist and banged his leg at every step.

He glanced back at her, then looked ahead again to watch where he was going. The stores in the mall had been packed with shoppers and there was a lot of traffic in the parking lot, all the cars driven by people with other things on their minds and with a heavy hand on the horn. And for good measure, there were still some patches of ice underfoot.

"Dave!" Patty called anxiously.

She saw him try to hitch his pile of packages more securely without smashing the shopping bag against the side of a parked car and without breaking his neck on the ice.

"Dave!" Patty called again. "I said, there's a man back there with red sand coming out of his ears, in that car we just passed!" Her arms were loaded with packages too and she was a little out of breath.

"Oh, for . . ." Dave muttered, loud enough for Patty to hear. He halted and looked around, trying to locate the Honda. It had grown dark outside while they were in the mall and now all the cars seemed to be the same color beneath the artificial lights of the parking lot.

As Patty caught up to him, Dave carefully propped the bundles against his knee and the door handle of a muddy station wagon, then gingerly rested his chin on top of the pile to keep it steady.

"What did you say?"

"I said, I just saw a man in a car with red sand coming out of his ears, just coming right out of his ears. In that car we just passed."

Dave closed his eyes for a second and adjusted his grip on the bundles. "Patty," he said, "we just passed about eight thousand cars."

"It's right back there. It's right in a straight line with where we're standing, sort of."

Dave made a point of looking past her shoulder. Patty saw that his face was wet with perspiration from the stifling heat in the stores.

He sighed, then said, "Where?"

"Right back there," Patty said at once. She pointed with her chin. "Back there, the way we just walked."

"Patty, there are about eight thousand cars between here and where we came out of the store."

The strain of a long Saturday spent shopping in the holiday crowds showed on Dave's face. He was trying his best to be patient, Patty knew, but she also knew that he must be thinking of all the overtime he'd have to put in just to bring home the money they'd spent today.

"Sand," he said.

Patty nodded and glanced back over her shoulder before meeting his eyes again.

"Red sand," Dave said.

"Red," Patty said. "Coming out of his ears." She knew she'd seen it.

"You're putting me on."

"Dave, really, I saw it. He was in the driver's seat with his head back against the thing, the head rest, and there was sand coming out of his ears. Well, his left ear anyway. It was falling on his shoulder, just sort of pouring out of his ear. I saw it clearly. It didn't register right away and we walked right past him, then I realized what it was. I saw it. I know I did."

Dave studied her face for a few seconds. "You're not kidding," he said.

"No, I'm not kidding! We should do something. Try to help or something, or tell somebody."

"Sand coming out of his ear," Dave said.

Patty nodded.

"Sand."

Patty felt the corners of her mouth begin to twitch a little. She knew she'd seen it but Dave didn't believe her. He was trying to be patient, but he was starting to look at her as if she were crazy.

"Honey, it was probably just a shadow you saw, that's all. It was just some guy sleeping in the car while the little woman spends all his money."

"I saw it, Dave. I . . . I just knew. I happened to glance in as we went by and . . . and I could just tell, that's all." But she lowered her gaze from her husband's face. Maybe she hadn't seen it, after all. But why would she imagine a thing like that?

"Patty, come on," Dave said, "I'm really knocked out. And I'm about to drop all this stuff any second now." He shivered as the perspiration on his face began to dry. "Come on, okay? Let's just make it back to the car, if we can even find it in all this mess." He was doing his best, Patty knew, to keep the impatience out of his voice. They had been married just under a year and a half, this was going to be their first Christmas in the new house and the first Christmas ever for the baby, Jennifer, and Dave showed all the time that he was madly in love with her. "Come on, babe," he said, and his voice sounded very gentle.

Now Patty was feeling uncertain. She glanced over her shoulder once more, looking back the way they had come. Some of the cars they'd passed had shifted positions, new ones maneuvering into spaces the instant they were vacated, and she was no longer certain of just exactly where it was she had seen the man with sand pouring out of his ears. If she had seen him at all. Maybe the hours of shopping and the crowds and the overheated stores had all been a bit much for her.

Dave lifted his bundles and did his best to settle them securely in his arms. He set off again, looking all around for the car.

God, Patty thought with a suddenness that took her breath away and brought a sinking feeling in her stomach, what a crazy thing to think! A man in a car with red sand coming out of his ears! Uh oh, better watch it, kiddo. Better lay off the holiday eggnog. And I better treat myself to a nap when we get home.

"Hey, Dave," she called, "wait up! What is it, a race?"

She caught up to him as he finished piling his packages on the ground beside their car and started fishing in his pocket for the keys. He found them after a moment, then blew on his frozen fingers to warm them. When he'd opened the trunk, he immediately took the packages out of Patty's arms and set them down inside. Then he turned to face her. He was smiling, looking once again like her gentle and loving husband.

"You had me going for a second there," he said. "Sorry I'm so crabby. Those stores just wipe me out."

Patty looked a little embarrassed. She felt her face flush. "I must have imagined it," she said. She brushed damp hair back from her face. "It must have just been the light or the shadows or something, I guess. I could have sworn it was sand."

Dave put on his most elaborately patient look, an expression that Patty particularly loved, and shook his head. "What am I going to do with you?" he said.

"Just love me, I guess," she answered. It was a little game they played, a warm and familiar ritual of dialogue.

Dave took her in his arms and they embraced, kissing right there in the parking lot. Somewhere nearby, little children giggled at them.

* * *

Christmas, their first Christmas in the new house and little Jennifer's first Christmas in the world, came and went with nothing but happiness and joy suitable to the season. They had decided many months before that, on New Year's Eve, they were going to stay home by themselves; they were going to be thoroughly selfish and share that special night, so filled with portent, only with each other. They did just that—little Jennifer obligingly slept soundly all through the night—and they enjoyed it every bit as much as they had expected.

They were both very happy—happy with themselves and happy with each other—and never once in those weeks of the holiday season did Patty even so much as remember the man in the car with red sand pouring out of his ears whom she had seen—*thought* she had seen—in the parking lot that night.

* * *

Then, on a Thursday evening during the last week of January, something happened that struck Patty as very strange.

Dave was working late, putting in some overtime. Patty loved him for that. She hated to see him coming in so late and so tired, but she knew he wanted to do it for her and Jennifer. He wanted to be able to give them the best of everything; where his family was concerned, no effort was too great. On nights when he worked late, Patty usually made spaghetti sauce for him. Her "famous spaghetti sauce," Dave called it. She made it just the way he liked, with plenty of oregano and red pepper mixed right in. The pot was simmering on the stove now.

Jennifer had turned out to be the best and quietest and most patient little darling in the world. She always ate without a fuss, didn't carry on if her meals were sometimes a little late, and slept all through the night. She was a strong and healthy baby too, with chubby arms and legs. Dave always said she'd be eating more spaghetti than he could himself in no time at all.

Patty carried Jennifer into the living room and sat her on the couch for a minute while she hurried back to the kitchen for the baby's dinner. Even though she wished Dave could be home on time every evening, Patty secretly loved these extra few hours by herself with the baby. "The girls' night," she called it in her thoughts.

She set the baby's food on the end table beside her and propped Jennifer up on her left leg. The TV was on and the six o'clock news was just starting.

Jennifer seemed to love this time too. She always sat so placidly on Patty's knee, eating her dinner with great gusto and watching the news with apparently the same interest as Patty. It could only be the moving images and the constantly changing colors that attracted her, but Patty liked to think, on "the girls' night," that the two of them were pals, two sleek, sophisticated women of the world, keeping up with the march of progress and the subtleties of political theories and international affairs. Besides, it was a good habit to establish from the very beginning with a baby; Patty had no intention of Jennifer's growing up to be an air-head.

They were about halfway through Jennifer's dinner and the baby was smiling happily at the screen and bouncing up and down a little with contentment when the TV anchorwoman put on her most serious expression and voice and launched into a report of a mysterious killing on Long Island.

There were no eyewitnesses to the killing, which had taken place in a suburban home in a quiet neighborhood. No one who lived on the street had heard a sound or suspected any foul play. A picture of a well-kept suburban home appeared on the screen. The anchorwoman reported that the crime was only discovered when a passerby had noticed a trail of red sand across a driveway. The screen showed a driveway and a neatly clipped lawn; dark red blotches marked the concrete. The passerby had grown suspicious and followed the trail of sand to some nearby bushes, where he had discovered the body of a man who had been stabbed six times with a carving knife. Apparently the man had crawled there after the attack. The anchorwoman appeared again on the screen. Police were investigating, she reported, and there was a possibility that the murder might be linked to some local gangland rivalry. The anchorwoman smiled warmly again. "We'll be back in a minute," she said, "to tell you why your dollar has been buying less food lately at the supermarket. Stay with us."

Patty stared at the screen. Her right hand, holding a spoonful of applesauce, was poised in the air halfway to Jennifer's mouth. The baby turned her head and looked curiously to see what had interrupted the flow of food. She watched her mother for a second, head cocked to one side, then turned back to the screen, where wrestler Hulk Hogan was warning the American public not to leave home without their American Express cards.

"A trail of red sand," the reporter had said. Patty had heard it clearly. And there was the picture of the driveway, in color. The sand on it, the red sand, had been unmistakable. Patty had seen it. The anchorwoman had not stressed it, had not made any special comment on it, but there was no mistaking the fact that what she had referred to was *sand.*

Patty put the spoonful of applesauce into Jennifer's mouth, bounced the baby a couple of times to remind her that Mommy loved her, and forced herself to continue feeding the baby the rest of the jar.

Sand. Red sand.

No, it wasn't possible.

Patty shook her head to clear away the cobwebs. Something crazy must have happened in her mind, just for that one moment. A mental short circuit or something. Obviously, her mind must have been wandering and had gone back to that silly thing that had happened in the mall parking lot just before Christmas. Patty hadn't thought of that again since the day it had happened, but it must have been lingering there at the back of her thoughts. Well, she told herself, things like that happened, odd thoughts coming together at random, without warning. It didn't mean anything. It just could not have been a trail of red *sand* that Long Island passerby had seen on the driveway. That didn't make sense.

She finished feeding Jennifer the applesauce—thank God for such a good baby, and with such a good appetite!—and then began getting Jennifer ready for the night. Patty took her time with it, enjoying the happy routine of the preparations, talking softly to Jennifer, hugging her tight and kissing her fat little nose. She loved an evening like this, "the girls' night," just the two of them.

She tucked Jennifer in carefully, taking her time about it, then sat down to watch her doze off. In a minute or two, the baby was sound asleep.

Red sand.

The thought was still lingering in her mind. But no, it couldn't mean anything. And Patty knew that if she told Dave about it, he would put on his patient face. For some reason, that old game didn't attract her tonight.

She went to the kitchen and cleaned up what was left of Jennifer's dinner, then treated herself to an extra cup of coffee.

Dave came in from work at a quarter after nine and Patty put the pasta on to boil. When he had worked his way through half a plate of spaghetti, he declared that the sauce was even better than usual. Patty remembered the item on the news, and the crazy thing she had thought she'd heard, but it just sounded too silly to her now and she said nothing of it to her husband.

* * *

Three weeks later, in the middle of February, something else happened.

It was a Saturday and Dave was working outside in the garage. He planned to build a deck at the back of the house as soon as the weather turned nice, and he'd already bought some of the lumber. When he had time on a weekend, he was always out in the garage with his beloved tools, studying the plans and cutting the lumber to the sizes he'd need. He kept promising the deck would be finished by the end of May so they'd have the use of it all summer, complete with screens to keep the mosquitoes away from Jennifer.

Suddenly he appeared in the kitchen doorway, his face white as a ghost.

For a second, he didn't say anything. Patty just stared at him.

"You've gotta drive me to the doctor," Dave said quickly. He was holding his left hand tightly with his right and pressing it against his chest. "I had a little accident. No big deal, but you have to get me to the doctor right away. I may need a stitch in my hand."

"What . . . ?"

Dave's face grew a little whiter. "Just a little accident," he said. He closed his eyes for a second. "Honey, c'mon, I need a doctor. I'll be okay, but I need a doctor."

Patty was staring at the steady stream of red sand that was trickling out of his hand and running down his shirt. Some of it caught on the top of his jeans and his belt buckle, and it was starting to gather on the floor at his feet. Patty could see it clearly. She could hear the gentle hiss as the stream hit the wooden steps outside the door. There was no mistaking the fact that it was sand.

"Dave!" she said as both the reality of his accident and the unreality of the sand coming from his wound struck her at the same time.

"Patty, I had an accident! *C'mon!*"

She ran for Jennifer, wrapped her up quickly, grabbed coats for herself and Dave, and had them all in the car in a minute or so. Later, she hardly remembered the drive to the nearest doctor's office.

In the waiting room, she played with Jennifer, more to keep herself occupied than to entertain the baby.

She had seen red sand trickling in a stream from Dave's hand where he had cut it with the saw.

She had seen no such thing.

All she wanted at the moment was for Dave to be all right. He was such a good guy, such a good husband and father, always working so hard to give them a better life. She hated to see him injured or in pain.

And she hated to see that sand pouring out of him.

No, that was wrong.

She hated—

Then Dr. Rosenstein was showing Dave out of his office, delivering him safely back to her. Patty planted Jennifer on her hip and rose to go to them. Dave's left hand was wrapped up tightly in a white bandage.

"He's going to be fine," the doctor was saying. "He'll be a little shy of a saw in the future, but he'll be fine. Nothing wrong that a couple of stitches can't cure. He'll be good as new in no time." He turned to

Dave, but his gaze included them both. "Now, you may get a little leaking from the wound for a day or two, but that's normal. Just a little sand trickling out at the edges, just a natural cleansing process. It's nothing at all to worry about. Just brush it off and forget about it. Of course, if you should have a lot of pain, give me a call right away. Otherwise, call me on Wednesday." He smiled broadly at them both. "Now you just go on home and take care of each other and that beautiful baby."

Patty fussed hugely over Dave for the rest of the day. She said nothing about the sand. Neither Dave nor the doctor had seemed to think there was anything odd or unusual about it, so . . .

But it *was* unusual. And odd. It was *sand.*

It could not have been sand. It simply could not.

For one crazy moment, she wondered if perhaps she had sand running in her own veins. But that thought was so obviously absurd that it made the whole episode of the afternoon seem incredibly silly.

She would just have to put such nonsense out of her mind. It wouldn't be easy, but she'd manage.

She said nothing to Dave about what she thought she'd seen.

* * *

On Tuesday of the following week, while she was peeling carrots for dinner, Patty cut her left index finger with the knife. It wasn't a bad cut, just a minor wound that barely penetrated the skin, but it bled profusely. She ran cold water on it at the sink for several minutes, and after a while the bleeding stopped.

It was only afterward, when she was peeling the rest of the carrots with a Band-Aid firmly in place on her finger, that she realized she'd been relieved to see the blood.

And two hours after that, Jennifer, who seldom had an accident of any sort, took a tumble off the couch and struck her head a grazing blow on the corner of the coffee table. She was such a good baby, so well-adjusted and secure, that she only cried briefly while Patty fussed over her to soothe her. The table had barely scraped her forehead, just enough to draw three tiny bright red pinpoints of blood, and Patty had it wiped and cleaned at once. Within minutes, Jennifer was back to her normal, happy self.

And again Patty had to admit, although she didn't even really want to think about it, that the sight earlier of her own blood and now of Jennifer's—perfectly normal, ordinary blood—had been a relief.

Well, so much for that.

* * *

Nothing odd happened during the rest of February or all through March.

But in April, in the first week alone, there were three incidents.

On that Monday afternoon, she was coming back from dropping Jennifer off at Grandma's. She parked the car in the driveway and was just pocketing the keys when she heard a child yell from the sidewalk in front of the next house. The yell was followed at once by terrified crying. Patty immediately ran toward where little Danny Paxton had fallen from his new bicycle. As she drew close to him, she could see that he didn't seem badly injured—he hadn't hit his head on the pavement or broken any limbs—but apparently he had scraped his knee very badly. His jeans were torn right across the knee and, as Patty knelt down beside the child, she could see that the skin was badly scraped and that red sand was trickling from a large, angry-looking abrasion on the head of the boy's kneecap.

In the same instant, Mrs. Paxton came running from the house, took in the scene at a glance, saw that her son was not badly injured, and gathered him up in her arms, thanking Patty at the same time for coming on the run. "Look at all this nasty sand," the woman said to her little boy as she cuddled him to soothe his fright. "We'll just have to go inside and brush it all away, won't we, and then you'll be good as new."

Patty was absolutely certain of it. She had seen the sand herself. No mistake: it was sand. And Mrs. Paxton had seen it. She had *said* it. And she had not thought there was anything unusual about it.

The next morning, while Patty was sitting at the dining room table, organizing the month's bills and writing checks, she cut the side of her right index finger on the edge of an envelope. A thin line of bright red blood welled up in the cut and Patty automatically raised the finger to her lips to lick it off. As she tasted the faint saltiness of it, she had a startling thought: I wonder if I'm normal.

On the Thursday afternoon of that same week, her mother called to say that she had just returned with Daddy from the Emergency Room of the hospital. Daddy had taken a bad spill on the back steps—no, thank God, he wasn't badly hurt, no bones broken or anything like that —but he'd hit the blade of a shovel with the back of his hand as he fell. "I never saw so much sand in all my life," Patty's mother said. "I was so frightened, I just raced him off to the hospital. It was just a bad scrape, just tore the skin pretty badly, but you know how I hate the sight of sand like that." Patty murmured something sympathetic and promised to call the next day to see how her father's hand was progressing.

She said nothing to Dave, or to anyone else, about any of these incidents.

But she did start keeping notes on anything of the sort that happened. They consisted just of the date and a word or two to remind her —"Daddy's hand," for instance—but, during the days while she and Jennifer were alone in the house, she spent a great deal of time staring at the list and worrying about herself and the baby.

* * *

May. June. July.

Patty's list had grown rapidly to several pages.

She kept them hidden at the bottom of her underwear drawer in the bedroom, but now she was taking the list out at least once a day and studying it, trying to find some pattern, some rhyme or reason, trying to make sense of it. But, as much as she pored over the entries on the list, every day, she could make no other sense of them than the obvious sense they made all by themselves.

No one in the world thought the sand was unusual except herself.

And the list kept growing longer.

They took a ride in the country on a Sunday afternoon. On a lonely road, just as Dave was slowing the car for a turn, Patty saw the body of a raccoon that had been struck and killed. It was at the edge of the pavement on her side and, with the car moving so slowly just then, she could not mistake the spray of red sand that surrounded the poor little thing's body. Patty reached for Jennifer in the baby seat beside her and began caressing the child's chubby little arm.

On the evening news on television, there was an announcement that local hospitals were appealing to the public to increase their donations of sand. Sand was always in short supply during the summer months, when the need was often greatest. After the announcement, Patty hugged Jennifer to her so tightly and for so long that even Jennifer, normally so yielding, began to squirm from her mother's embrace.

The list of incidents kept growing, and, each time she made an entry, Patty gathered up Jennifer and examined her closely. She looked at the child's skin, tried to trace the lines of veins and arteries, studied the child's pink cheeks and the inside of her eyes. The child *seemed* normal enough, but as Patty's list grew longer and longer, she became more and more worried about both herself and her child.

Then, on an afternoon in the last week of July, everything was finally settled in her mind. She and Jennifer were having lunch. Jennifer had been growing by leaps and bounds and was curious now about everything and snatching at all sorts of things with her fat little hands. Before Patty could stop her on this occasion, Jennifer reached out at the table and grabbed the fork from Patty's plate. But she grabbed it firmly by the tines and the point of one punctured the ball of her thumb. Blood bubbled up from the wound and dripped onto the table as Jennifer began an unaccustomed round of loud and pitiable crying.

That was it.

Patty cleaned and bound up the wound, then hurried herself and Jennifer into the car. She knew just where she had to go.

In little more than an hour, they were home again. Patty had not been able to get exactly what she needed, but this was an emergency and what she had with her now would have to do until she could get precisely the right thing.

She moved quickly, anxious to do what had to be done now that she finally saw it all clearly.

On a chair beside the dining room table she set the biggest pot she had, the one she always used for Dave's spaghetti. Then she opened three of the bags she'd bought and emptied them into the pot. As she worked, her mind was racing. God, she thought, I should have done this long ago.

She folded a blanket on the surface of the table, lifted up a curious Jennifer, stripped off the baby's clothes, and placed her on her back on the blanket. Jennifer made some incomprehensible sound and watched her mother closely.

Despite her hurry, Patty felt infinitely better, now that she saw everything clearly and knew exactly what she was doing.

Red gravel from the pet shop wasn't exactly the right thing, but it would do in an emergency. Later, she would find red sand of exactly the right consistency, but the gravel was better than nothing.

Patty had to use all the force of her love for Jennifer, but after a moment and a few deep breaths, she was able to keep her hand steady enough for the first incision. After that it was easy. It only took a couple of minutes to get out all the messy wet stuff from inside and replace it with heaping handfuls of the gravel. She'd have to get the proper kind of sand as quickly as possible, she knew that, but the gravel would do as an emergency measure. Patty loved Jennifer so much, she just couldn't let things go a single day longer. And Jennifer was such a good baby. She hardly cried at all while Patty worked.

In only a few minutes, she was finished with the baby.

Then, with a wonderful sense of relief, Patty went to work on herself.

THE BLUE MAN

by Terry L. Parkinson

The rustling of paper. The paper flies from the desk, floats above his heavy head like a cloud. His elbow slips from the edge, and his face slaps the surface.

Curtis lifts bleary eyes to see the paper fall lazily to the ground. Still half-caught in dream, he puts inert hands to his face, feeling for the bones beneath his flesh. He peers about, his eyes slowly coming into focus. The room shimmers, then solidifies.

He moves, like a compass opening, tracing an arc to the other side of the room. There, he is away from the seat of his troubling dreams. There, he is not required to ponder the age-old pursuit.

The lamp is on, and the room basks in the yellow glow. Shadows are indistinct. He surveys the room: mushroom-shaped lamp, end table obscured by forest-green couch, tangible blue lucite coffee table verified by yesterday's newspaper and several unread books, soft amber carpet which hushes footsteps. Translucent curtains wave in an unfelt breeze.

Curtis replaces the books on the bookshelf. He folds the newspaper and places it in the wicker basket next to the fireplace.

He bolts the front door; looks out the tiny porthole (rubbing the knots from his tensed shoulders); sees only dark, and the shimmering trace of the sidewalk to the street.

He lights a cigarette and falls into the waiting imprint of himself in his favorite armchair (a jungle of black and green flowers). He stares at the sleeping television, props his feet on the table to frame it, then flicks on the set with a red toe that pokes through a hole in his blue sock.

The room now sizzles with animation. Curtis falls farther back into the chair, barely noticing the images that hold his attention.

Somewhere behind the line of images, a voice calls. A deadly familiar voice, half-heard. Curtis concentrates on the roar coming from the screen, hoping that it will drown out the voice.

Apparently he is successful, for suddenly the room is stripped of color. A white blizzard moves about the walls, like a swarm of insect shadows thrown by moonlight. Curtis smiles, not allowing himself to feel startled; he has fallen asleep again, and the station has gone off the air. He feels the familiar yet illicit tingle of having fallen asleep outside of bed, and waking in uncertain circumstances.

He kicks the switch and the room darkens.

It is then that he hears the first sound. Out of nothing it springs. The bushes rustle outside the front window, a gentle sound that could be wind, that strengthens into the frenetic, angular sound of pursuit.

Curtis sits rigidly in the inherited chair, Grandfather's chair (now recovered), not daring to blink, hoping therefore to be unobserved. His left thigh cramps, but he dares not move or else he will be . . . seen.

The glass smudges, a cloud of breath. But soon a child's greasy fingerprints appear. The whorls grow, patterned like windblown sand. Then two adult hands appear, with the absences between the fleshy parts, that are the lines, by which a life can be told.

Behind their signature, two blue hands emerge, grow backward into arms, a torso (which shimmers and stops, shimmers and stops, leaving a trail of afterimages), and two legs. The feet hide in grass. The headless ghost pulls the afterimages into its center, and begins to grow a neck. Curtis bolts from his chair.

He knows what's next. Reasonably, he turns away. Now he knows nothing.

Back turned, he stares at the dark walls, the paintings he cherishes invisible in the night of the room. The Miró sketch is there—third from the right—two thousand dollars last month. Two balloons, a yellow and a red, and one string.

The ghost grows a face. Curtis hears it knock against the glass: a windblown face.

He recalls, standing still with his back to the window, the time when the ghost had first appeared, when he was seven years old. One still summer night when the crickets screamed a single note, it had rushed out of a corner: the corner wished to speak, and a mouth had risen and spoken. A face followed, held in the air by a trailing snake-like body.

Had he ever seen the face? He cannot now call it to mind. He had paced the foot of his bed that night (and on subsequent nights), hoping to crush out the memory of the apparition. His parents had been unable to wake him; finally, they had put him, fully clothed, into a shower, and that had brought him back out of the nightmare of himself.

After that first encounter, the blue man, who was ever after his constant if seldom seen companion, who grew in his school desk, who carved space out of water in public showers but which no one else could see, who lived next door in the dorm as a cloak for a silent man, and in a woman he had loved whose irises contained the reflection of the pursuing ghost; after the first encounter he would never look the ghost in the face, for it wore many guises and the terror of it would force Curtis' eyes closed. The ghost had resorted to many tricks to make inroads into his conscious mind, but Curtis prided himself on his ability to outwit it. In fact, it had become a sort of self-effacing game, this well-flexed ability to turn away from anything, at the merest of indications.

Yet it had followed him here, into the heart of this anonymous suburb, the perfect hideout, where Curtis lived sedately and with as little drama as possible, to deter the pursuit, for, as he surmised, if he was not on his own path, then no one, or nothing, could easily follow.

Curtis rubs his cramped thigh, and is brought out of this reverie. There is only faint light, but it is enough. In the glass covering one photograph (the photographer's self-portrait, a face half-clear and half-blurry), he sees the blue reflection of the ghost, who is now full-grown, man-sized, complete with head atop a neck overly long and quizzical, perhaps distorted by the two panes of glass, the window behind and the pane before. The feet are invisible, cut off by the frame into which Curtis stares.

Curtis is compelled to peer over his shoulder; his neck tenses against the effort.

The ghost responds to the hesitant turning. The two blue hands, grown large and somehow poignant, slide down the glass, a cry issuing from the glass like the plea of a hurt child, heard from across a great distance.

The hands fall below the frame.

Curtis turns to the window. The hands disintegrate into smoke, and fly separately toward the dark trees, a broken prayer beneath a half-moon that moves in and out of clouds.

It is too late, too late.

The visitation is over.

Curtis turns uneasily in his sleep. He wakes in the middle of the night; it is three o'clock.

He pulls on his robe, and paces around his bed. The room is small and damp. An oily night breeze stirs through the slot-like window, a faint promise of endless space.

He pulls on his clothes. He cannot rest. There had been a party. Crowds of people unnerve his sleep. The edges of the room, although dark, have a razor clarity, as though the room is carved from black steel.

Curtis moves through the front door, brushing imagined cobwebs from his face. The door self-locks behind him. He does not throw the bolt (for the key is still inside); he is safe, unseen, alone.

Two days past full, the moon moves toward the field of stars.

The street, slick and black, is a snake trailing to a distance unknown in the dark, overly familiar in the day.

He places his feet hesitantly on the asphalt, which simultaneously loses its reflective quality; romance collapses like an empty suit of clothes.

Curtis closes his eyes. The wind whispers through trees, cutting like a scythe.

He smells an intoxicating vapor, flowers of some sort, the source of which he has never been able to determine.

One foot after the other, and he walks on, past Ralph's house, past April's house (April suffers from Alzheimer's disease), and others; the houses are empty. Everyone is in bed, gone, perhaps dreaming of themselves as children, looking for salamanders beneath stones, and finding their own faces.

Curtis imagines April drooling on her pillow.

He wonders, slowly opening his eyes, if spring has ever touched this land. Spring is an event on a calendar. The dry street seems endless.

He reaches the bend of the road, where the houses end. A quarter of a mile of road lies ahead, peppered with shadows of a few houses in various stages of construction. Beyond, only empty road.

Night fills this road; wind rushes between two invisible walls.

He hurries along. His feet echo; he increases his pace still more. Is he being followed? He risks a glance behind. Nothing, save for his unseen historical footprints.

The echoes continue, another set of footsteps pounding off wet stone. The two rhythms beat out an eerie resonance. He feels the beat in his ears, in the pulse in his stomach.

Soon he reaches the brick wall at the end of the road, and the drumbeat of multiplying footsteps ceases. He reassures himself that the echoes have issued from this excavated wall of an underground conduit.

He searches for a foothold on the wall, which is vaguely slippery in the night air, finds a precarious handhold instead, and pulls himself up. Level with the top of the brick wall, like a roofless second story, is a dark field of recently felled trees that are like cannon after a battle.

Curtis pushes past the sign that tells the name of the contractor of this as yet unbuilt subdivision. Curtis nervously peers at the road below, the road behind, for he worries, now that his feet are on higher ground than his home, that he might be seen.

Curtis sees nothing, although his vision blurs. He wipes at his eyes. The myopic arc of light disappears. The warm glove of night is everything; it is enough.

Curtis moves into the field, beyond which lie despondent hills scrubbed of vegetation by the insistent wind.

As he walks, Curtis removes his clothes, piece by piece, desiring to be clothed only by the warm wind.

The hairs on his spine rise as the wind licks his back; his shirt drops to the ground. He kicks off his shoes, which arc in different directions; the grass and stone, the fingers and hand of the earth touch him. The wind tugs at his fly, and blood flows into his groin. He pushes out, past the growing obstacle, and moves out of his pants in a single deliberate motion.

He runs heavily veined hands down his moonlit body, a felt figure reflected from the television screen. The edges of his human life, determined and angular, are apparent now under his hands. This is the superstructure on which his life is built, the subdivision of himself.

He walks on in a state of ecstasy.

Can anyone see me? I would like someone to see me.

He reaches the center of the field, compelled by the river of wind. He looks to his feet, which are now masked by shadow. Desiring to feel the ground more fully, he kneels, stumbling in the effort. His vision is turned momentarily backward in the arc of this accident, to the edge of the field.

There stands another moonlit man, clothed, fully footed and face forward, penetrating Curtis' ecstasy with a hard, cold gaze. The eyes, even at this distance, contain a clear message. They express the fulfilled longing of half a life, the cold light of the moon filtered through a dazed mind—their intention is dangerously apparent.

The blue man pivots, and disappears over the edge.

Curtis raises a bruised knee from the ground, and rushes back toward the wall, leaping over trees, retrieving what clothes he can. Shirt wrapped about his waist, pants in hand, and wearing one shoe, he leaps down the wall, landing on his bare foot.

The blue man runs ahead, fully formed and without a shimmer, a block distant.

Curtis surges with panic, and accelerates, forgetting his torn feet. They leave a bloody trail; are worn away by the pavement.

He rounds the bend in the road, coming back into the line of occupied houses. The night is stripped; the fog has entered unnoticed, and the sky whitens into a false dawn.

The blue man turns into the walkway that leads to Curtis' front door.

Curtis reaches the walk an eternity later, each footfall tracing an unbearably long arc.

He leaps to the front porch like a maddened animal, unreasonably grabbing the doorknob. The door is locked. He himself had locked it, an eternity ago. He fumbles for his keys, which elude his frantic fingers, but he finally manages to fit the slippery key into the lock and turn it.

The blue man has disappeared.

The lock clicks, but the door remains closed fast. Curtis furiously turns the key, which bends; pulls back from his frenzy for a moment to consider.

Knowing his door only too well, he realizes that the deadlock has been thrown from the inside.

He throws the useless keys into the garden.

Curtis collapses, weeping, to the ground. He looks up with blurry eyes to the white sky, which offers no solace.

He crawls through the rosebushes to the front window. There, he sees the blue man sitting in his favorite chair, in human form, in the shape of Curtis' life.

Curtis raises ghostly blue hands, imploringly, to the glass. But his turn is over.

The man inside stands up.

And looks away.

A DEMON IN ROSEWOOD

by Sharon Webb

The boy did not notice the demon until early evening. At first it had been fun to lie in the antique French bed in the guest room and watch the fire flickering in the old Franklin stove. By the last of the day's gray light, he could see the rain fall and cling in frozen beads to the bare gray dogwood outside the window.

Jason gave a tug to the thick blue-and-white quilt that covered him. It slid in his grasp, exposing his right foot, heavy in its plaster cast. He tentatively wiggled the toes that emerged from the padded open end. The ache was remote now, dulled by the blue-and-gray capsule his mother had given him when he had begun to cry with the pain.

They had brought him home from the emergency room early that afternoon. He had cried then too, partly because of the jarring pain in his ankle when the car jumped and jolted over the rutted gravel road, partly because of Big Red. "Will you go look for him, Daddy? Will you?" Tears streaked his face as he struggled to push himself up on his elbows.

His mother reached back over the seat of the car and stroked his hair —Jason's golden fleece, she always called it. "Lie still, honey. And keep your foot up so it won't swell." She exchanged a look with her husband, who said lightly, "Maybe Big Red will be waiting for us."

But the porch of the old farmhouse that they called home now was empty. Jason listened for the greeting bark of the big Irish Setter, listened for the thud of his clown's feet dancing across the porch, but all he heard was the cry of the wind in the gray trees.

The damp wind cut through his clothes and he shivered as his father took him in his arms and carried him toward the house. A fat drop of rain splatted against Jason's cheek and slid like another tear down his face, "Please look for him, Daddy."

But his father was scanning the sky just then and not the woods that tumbled in stark winter grays and browns down the ravine that plunged away from the house. "It's starting," he said to his wife, who stepped ahead and opened the door for them. "We're going to have an ice storm."

He carried the boy into the house and down the hall—the old dog-trot, he called it. "We're going to put you in the guest room tonight, Jase. If the power goes off, it'll be warmer here than in your room. We don't want you catching cold."

"I'm afraid he already has," said his mother. She brushed away a tumbled blond lock of hair from Jason's forehead and settled cool fingers there. "He feels warm. Do you feel hot, honey?"

She was answered by a vigorous shake of the head and a cough. "All we need is the flu," she said with a look toward her husband. "And no wonder. Lying soaked in the bottom of the ravine for who knows how long?" Then to the boy: "It's vitamin C time, young man."

While his mother hurried off to the medicine chest, Jason's father ensconced the boy on the old rosewood bed, propped him with four pillows—two for his head and two to raise his ankle—and then began to lay a fire in the stove. Backing it with two logs, he kindled the fire with feathered strips of newspaper and a fat knot of pine. When it blazed, a few judicious jabs with the lion-head poker sent licking orange flames through the crevices of the split oak he laid on top. "There," he said. Satisfied, he returned the brass poker to its rack with a rattling clink as a sudden gust of wind sent the smell of woodsmoke into the room.

"Daddy?" The boy's unspoken question hung between them. The boy watched his father pull on the heavy plaid jacket once again. "I'll look for him now, son."

Drowsy from the warmth of the thick quilt and the fire, Jason picked at the light supper his mother brought, and afterward tried to solve the wooden puzzle she brought him, but the game was no match for the combination of fatigue and pain pill. The puzzle pieces fell from his hands and he slept.

His sleep was uneasy. The wind scurried through dead leaves and moaned in the rafters of the old house. The sound interposed itself in his dream and he heard the wind as his own footsteps at the edge of the ravine. He had been running up hillsides, sliding down gullies on the worn seat of brown corduroy pants, as he followed his dog on a joyous Saturday-morning romp through the woods. Out of breath, he clung to a branch, steadying himself. Far below, Big Red paused once to lap from a tiny splashing stream and then followed the tumbling brook downward until both disappeared in a dark green thicket of laurel.

At the crack of a rifle and its echoing whine, the boy's head went up. When it was answered by a sudden yelping scream from below, Jason froze for a tortured second. Then he was scrambling downward, half running, half falling, grabbing for handholds until a rotten branch snapped under his fingers and sent him plunging to the floor of the leaf-slick ravine.

The stabbing pain in his ankle stole his breath. He lay with fists clenched, silent in his agony until the worst of it was over. Then he was able to cry—a whimpering, helpless cry at the throb of a broken bone and the sharper pain of the dark red splash of blood that was not his own.

A drizzling rain came then. It came from a sky the color of lead that darkened the bare woods to grays and blacks and a single splash of blood red that thinned and dribbled in lurid streaks into the charcoal earth.

It was so cold. So cold. He shivered and tried to draw himself into a ball. The movement hurt his ankle and he whimpered. Hands touched his shoulders, his brow. "Jason? Jase. Wake up." His mother stood over him, light from the oak fire flickering on her hair. She turned on the bedside lamp and he saw that she had a thermometer in her hand. "Can you hold this in your mouth?" He nodded and she slipped it under his tongue. It was slim and cold and tasted faintly of alcohol. When she took it out and turned it under the light to read the thin silver line, her brow knitted, then smoothed as she looked at him. "I think I'd better get you some aspirin, sport."

He could hear her in the other room, dialing the phone, then talking quietly. By the time she came back with the aspirin he was chilled again. He shook his head at the tall glass of apple juice she offered.

"Try to drink it, honey. I called your doctor and she said to force fluids."

His teeth chattered against the rim of the glass as he tried to drink. "C-cold," he managed to say.

She looked uncertain for a moment, and then turned and pulled another quilt from the chest at the foot of the bed. As she spread it over him, tucking it around his shoulders, she said, "I guess I really shouldn't cover you up like this, but it's awful to be shivery." She leaned over to give him a kiss but instead gave a startled jump backward as an ice-laden branch outside the window broke with a sharp crack and crashed to the ground. "Oh, no! The old hickory." She ran to the window and stared out. Across the creek, an answering crack, and a post oak split in two—jagged splinters of wood, ice-pale on gray. "He shouldn't be out in this," she said, throwing open the window, calling to her husband. She was answered by a whisper of cold wind. Calling again, she tapped her fingers against the sill and stared out at the flat gray remnants of evening for a moment longer before she shut the window.

The lights went out abruptly. "I'll get the lamps," she said, moving toward the door.

With pupils widening in the dim light, he stared around the room. Shadows crouched in the corners, blurring them, making the room seem huge with only a tiny splash of light to hold back the pressing darkness. Suddenly he blinked. Something moved—something on the oiled doors of the old rosewood armoire that stood like a sentinel to the right of the tall bed. But the movement wasn't on the surface at all; it seemed to come from just inside, as if the shiny finish were a dim, streaked glass—a window.

The armoire was a massive piece, too tall for a modern, low-ceilinged house. Even here, its dark scrolls stretched curving horns toward the shadowy angle where wall met cornice, where cornice touched ceiling. He stared at the tall doors that squatted above wide drawers. Firelight flickered across the grain of the wood, and again the light red streaks of the rosewood seemed to move within the dark matrix.

Uneasy, the boy turned eyes bright with fever toward the stove and the hypnotic flames that licked the blackened logs. He lay half asleep for a time until a prickling began at the nape of his neck. For a moment he was afraid to look, but the armoire pulled his eyes like a magnet. The piece had been carefully made. Its doors, meeting with scarcely a seam, showed perfectly matched, perfectly symmetrical patterns of light red grain against a dark, almost black, background. And there was something else, something in the fire-red whorls and curving streaks. He stared at the polished doors. Again the movement—almost imperceptible in the shadows. It was then that he noticed the twin knots that blazed like slanting eyes.

He stared. From the center of each coal-red knot, dark pupils glittered in the firelight. Behind them, something writhed, and for a flashing instant Jason felt himself pulled toward it. With a start, he clung to the thick quilt as if it could serve as an anchor.

The suggestion of a mouth twisted across the rosewood surface. A blood-red smile slithered on serpent's coils, then vanished. . . . The eyes again. Shivering with a brightening chill, he stared at them—at the brows that arched above them and darkened into hard, curving points.

Blinking, he tried to look away, tried to fix his gaze on something else, but, each time, he found himself drawn back to the fiery eyes. It's not anything, he told himself. It was like seeing things in clouds—things that weren't really there. "It's just a piece of wood," he said aloud, but softly, under his breath, as if he were afraid that someone—something—would overhear.

A frozen branch made rat scratches on the roof as a gust of winter breathed through the window cracks. Splinters of ice crawled along his spine when he heard—he was sure he heard—a harsh sigh answer the wind. The scent of lemon oil struck his nostrils, a scent that masked a fainter, sharper odor that hovered just beyond it. Against his will, he felt his eyes drag toward the armoire again, felt them lock with coal-red eyes that seemed to stare inside his soul.

Black pupils fixed on his . . . glittering serpent's pupils dilating. . . . For a hideous moment he saw what coiled inside.

His lips moved, forming the silent word "Mama." Over and over they moved, but no sound escaped them, until he found the breath to scream.

Oblivious to the ice crystals that still clung to the rough wool jacket, Jason pressed closer to his daddy's chest, and shook his head. "I'm not afraid. I'm not." He gave an anxious glance toward the armoire, then looked quickly away.

"Anybody might see things in a piece of rosewood furniture, Jase. Even grown-ups."

The boy fixed doubting gray eyes on his father's. "Yeah?"

"Do you know why?"

He shook his head again.

"Well, rosewood is a different sort of wood. It grows in the tropics—and it grows very fast, but there's not much of it, so it's expensive. The reason there's not much of it is that by the time a rosewood is big enough to harvest, there isn't any heartwood left. It's gone—the heart has rotted away." He paused for a moment to caress the boy's hair. "So they take the outer part of the tree and slice it into very thin layers." He gently turned the boy's head in the direction of the armoire. "The 'eyes' you saw are just a place where a branch grew, Jason—two eyes, because you're looking at different layers of the same branch set side by side."

Jason swallowed, then stared at the armoire. It did look different in the bright light from the kerosene lantern his father had set on the bedside table. Besides, didn't his daddy know all about wood? Architects had to. He glanced up as his mother came into the room and looked at him with anxious eyes. "Better now?"

"Much better," said his father, "huh, Jason?"

The boy managed a grin.

"I brought you some company."

She held a brandy snifter—home of his pet Siamese fighting fish.

"I thought Thai-Dye might be getting chilly up in your room," she said, cradling the snifter between her palms as if to give it warmth. "It's a mite nippy up there with the power off." She looked at the fish. "Maybe he needs a warm bath." The blood-red betta hung motionless for a moment and then swam to the surface, as he did periodically, for a swallow of air. "I guess he's all right," she said and placed the snifter on the table next to the bed.

"And now I think it's bedtime for both of you," she said briskly. "It's been too long a day." She leaned over him. "Kiss goodnight?"

He clung to her a shade longer than usual. Then he said, "It's cold outside too. Big Red'll be cold out there."

Her eyes clouded for a second and she looked at her husband, then back at Jason. "Maybe he's waiting out the storm in a cave somewhere, Jase. Maybe he'll turn up in the morning."

They took away the kerosene lamp and its bright circle of light and left him alone then. The boy carefully avoided the twin doors of the armoire. "Just a branch," he whispered. "Daddy said." But still, it seemed better not to look. Instead, he watched the betta circle its tiny prison, watched it swim out of sight then suddenly reappear, its trailing blood-red fins magnified by the curves of the glass.

At the corner of his eye something wavered on the surface of the wide drawer beneath the armoire's twin doors—a curving red plume twitching in the shadows. He stared anxiously. Then he almost laughed. It was a tail, a feathery red tail. Big Red. He was all right! All right now. Jason raised himself on one elbow in order to see better in the flickering light of the fire until a quick fit of coughing exhausted him and he sank back against the pillows.

The feathery movements of the fire-red tail combined with the swirl of the betta at the edge of his vision. Suddenly his eyes blurred and he felt quite dizzy. He rubbed his eyes with both fists until a sheet of fire burned behind his closed lids. A whisper tickled against his ear and he clawed at it. A streak of blood stained his nails.

He anchored his gaze in a pint of water. The distortion of the snifter hid the betta. He could see nothing in the water but a pebble magnified to boulder size and a giant fernlike drift of milfoil. Then slowly, very slowly, the betta rolled into view, its huge body listing to one side like a crippled, sinking ship, its closed fins trailing like dark dripping splotches of blood. Glassy shark eyes stared at his.

He blinked and looked away as a muttered whisper pressed against his ear. The heavy scent of lemon oil crept into his nostrils, clogging them, making it hard for him to take in air. He threw back his head and tried to get his breath, but the air was hot and foul.

Something swam on the surface of the wide drawer. A blood-red betta floated in a fiery rosewood sea. The veil of its fins moved. A window opened.

The fleshy rags of its rotting demon heart beat against his mind and he knew then what it wanted. He felt it waiting, testing scraps of chilled and weakened flesh, discarding those that were not suitable. He felt it waiting with arch smile and infinite patience. And with curling horror, he felt his unwilling eyes rise to meet its flaming stare.

"We've got to get him to the hospital." Jason's mother sat on the tall bed and clung to the boy. He lay still now, his eyes almost focusing on theirs, yet his fingers still dug into the blue-and-white quilt as if to let go would be to die. "He's burning up."

The boy's father stared at her, a worried frown creasing his brow. "I don't see how." He glanced toward the dark window that reflected the guttering lamplight like a blind eye. "The road is greased glass by now. There's no way we can get out without chains."

"And why don't we have them?" Shrillness edged her voice. "For God's sake, why don't we have them?"

His eyes narrowed at her attack. "Because I'm a stupid fool, I guess. Or maybe I'm a dangerous psychotic who wants to endanger his own son."

Lips clamped, she thrust her chin away from him. But in a moment, the stiffness left her body and her hand fluttered toward her mouth. "What are we going to do? No phone— No way to get help—"

He stared helplessly at his wife and child for a moment. Then he scooped up the boy in a heavy layer of quilt and blankets and turned toward the door.

"Where are you going? Where are you taking him?"

"Out of here." He stalked up the hall, trailing bed clothes behind him. She followed in time to see him lay the boy gently in their own bed.

Jason's lips moved. His father bent to catch the faint sound. Then he held the boy close, patting him, saying, "No it isn't. Everything's all right now. Everything's OK."

The light from the lamp and the open fireplace danced on the white paneled walls of the bedroom and warmed it with yellows and touches of orange. Gradually, the boy's body relaxed and his fingers loosed their anchoring grip on the quilt.

"He's asleep," said his father.

The worried furrows smoothed away from his mother's brow. "Poor little guy. He's had a hellish day."

They stood and watched him in silence for a few minutes. Then her fingers touched his brow. "His fever's broken. I think he'll rest now."

"It might not be a bad idea for you and me to do the same," he said, nodding toward the door. "I guess it's the guest room for you and me— in the interest of warmth."

They smoothed the tumbled rosewood bed and put out the lamp. She lay in the bed and stared up at the shadowy armoire and then said to her husband, "It is a little spooky in this light . . . and with a fever," she added, "no wonder he was seeing things."

He nodded drowsily. "I can see the eyes he was talking about." He reached out and touched her hand as red lights moved on the surface of the armoire. "It's funny," he said. "I can almost make out a face there."

"I see it too," she said, her pupils widening in the darkness. Then her fingers tightened against his, "What did he say to you back there in our room?"

"Huh?"

"What did he say?"

"Oh," answered the sleepy voice. "He said, 'Too late. It's too late.'" And as her nails dug painfully into his hand he yelped. "What are you doing?" But she was staring at the armoire. "Look at it. The face— Oh, God! It looks like Jason." And then she was out of the bed, running down the hall, her heart fluttering like a wild thing.

At the door she hung back for a second, eyes squeezed shut. Oh, please God let him be all right. Please, God.

Fighting a blind panic, she scurried to the bedside of her son.

He lay sleeping, his cheek cradled in a chubby hand, his hair deep gold in the firelight.

Limp with relief, she steadied herself against the bedpost and caught her breath. And when a smile trailed across the sleeping child's face, she felt its trembling echo on her own.

Scamp, she thought. Little devil, to scare your mama like that. She reached out a hand and caressed the coiling tendrils of his hair. And at her touch he smiled again and opened coal-red eyes.

WISH

by Al Sarrantonio

Christmas.

A baby-blanket of snow enfolded the earth, nuzzled the streets. Great lips of snow hung from gutters, caps of snow topped mailboxes and lampposts.

Christmas.

Dark green fir trees stood on corners, heavy with ornaments and blinking bulbs, dusted with silver tinsel that hung from each branch like angels' hair. Great thick round wreaths, fat red bows under their chins, hung flat against each door. Telephone poles sprouted gold stars; more lights, round fat and bright, were strung from pole to pole in parallel lines. The air, clean and cold as huffing breath, smelled of snow, was white and heavy and fat with snow.

Christmas.

Christmas was here.

It was April.

Daisy and Timothy hid tight in the cellar. Tied and dusty, April surrounded them in fly-specked seed packets, boxes of impotent tulip bulbs, rows of limp hoes and shovels. Spring was captured and caged, pushed flat into the ground and frozen over, coffined tight and dead.

Above them, out in the world, they heard the bells. A cold wind hissed past. The cellar window shadowed over as something slid past on the street.

Ching-ching-ching.

They held their breaths.

Ching-ching.

The window unshadowed; the hiss and bells moved away.

The bells faded to a distant rustle.

They breathed.

Timothy shook out a sob.

"Don't you touch me!" he bellowed when his sister put a hand on his shoulder. "It's your fault! All the rest are in that *place* because of you—don't you *touch* me!" He pushed himself farther back between two boxes marked "Beach Toys."

Outside, somewhere, a mechanical calliope began to play "Joy to the World."

Winter silence hung between them until Timothy said, "I'm sorry."

Daisy held her hand out to him, her eyes huge and lonely, haunted. He did nothing—but again when her fingers fell on his shoulder he recoiled.

"No! You wished it! It's your fault!"

Daisy hugged herself.

Timothy's face was taut with fright. "You said, 'I wish it was Christmas always! I wish this moment would last forever!' " He pointed an accusing hand at her. "I was there when you said it. By the fireplace, while we hung our stockings. I heard that voice too—*but I didn't listen to it!*" He pointed again. *"Why did you have to wish?"*

"I wish it was April! I wish it was spring!" Daisy screamed, standing up. An open carton of watermelon seeds, collected carefully by the two of them the previous summer, tilted and fell to the floor. Unborn watermelons scattered dryly everywhere. "It was just a voice, I don't know how it happened," she sobbed. *"I wish it was Spring!"*

Nothing happened.

Outside the frosted cellar window, the calliope finished "Joy to the World" and went without pause into "Silver Bells."

"You wished it and now you can't unwish it!" Timothy railed. "That voice is gone and now it will always be Christmas!"

Daisy's face changed—she ignored his squirming protest when she clamped her hand to his arm.

"Listen!" she whispered fiercely.

"I won't! It's your fault!"

"Listen!"

Her wild, hopeful eyes made him listen.

He heard nothing for a moment. There was only Christmas winter out there—a far-off tinkly machine playing Supermarket carols, the sound of glass ornaments pinging gently against one another on out-door trees and, somewhere far off, the sound of bells.

But then there was something else.

Warm.

High overhead.

Blue and yellow.

A bird.

Daisy and Timothy raced for the window. Daisy got there first, but Timothy muscled her away, using the pulled cuff of his flannel shirt to rub-melt the frost from a corner of the rectangular glass. He put his eye to the hole.

Listened.

Nothing; then—

Birdsong.

He looked back at his sister, who pulled him from his peephole and glued herself to it. After a moment—

"I see it!"

Mountain-high overhead, a dark speck circled questioningly.

It was not a Christmas bird. It had nothing to do with Christmas. It was a spring bird, seeking April places—green tree branches and brown moist ground with fat red worms in it. A sun yellow and tart-sweet as lemons. Mown grass with wet odors squeezed out of each blade. Brown-orange baseball diamonds and fresh-blacktopped playfields smelling of tar.

The bird whistled.

"April!" Timothy shouted.

He pulled frantically at the latch to the window, turning it aside and pulling the glass panel back with a winter groan. Cold air bit in at them. Snow brushed at their foreheads, danced and settled in their hair.

Timothy climbed out.

High up, whirling like a ball on a string, the bird cried.

"Yes! Yes! Spring!" Timothy yelled up at it.

Daisy climbed out beside him.

"You did it!" Timothy said happily. "You undid your wish!"

The cellar window snapped shut.

Something small plummeted.

Frozen white and silver, the bird fell into a soft death-coverlet of snow.

"It was a trick!" Timothy screamed. "What are we going to do?" He turned to the locked window, tried frantically to push it in. When he opened his mouth, puffs of frosted air came out with his words.

"We've got to get away!"

Timothy and Daisy looked to the horizon. A huge red ball was there, a second sun, an ornament a hundred stories high, and from it came the faint jangle of bells, the smooth snow-brushed sound of sleigh runners.

"We'll be brought to that place—we've got to get away!"

The sleigh bells, the glassy sound of sled-packed snow, grew toward them. Before Daisy's hands could find Timothy, could pull him against the side of the house, he tore away from her. The bells rose to a hungry clang; Daisy could almost hear them sing with pleasure.

Timothy's fading voice called back:

"Why did you listen to that voice . . ."

The bells grew very loud and then very soft, and moved away.

Christmas continued. In the sky, a few hearty snowflakes pirouetted and dropped. Tinsel shimmered on tree branches. The air stayed clean and cold, newly winterized. Balsam scent tickled the nostrils. Christmas lights glowed, blinked.

From the horizon, from the giant red Christmas ball, came a sound.
Bells.
Soft silver bells.

"No!" Daisy's feet carried her from the side of the house to the white-covered sidewalk. She left tiny white feet in a path behind her.

The bells belled.

Daisy ran.

The lazy bells followed her. Like a ghost's smoky hands, they reached out at her only to melt away and re-form. Daisy passed snow-white houses, with angels in the windows and mistletoe under the eaves.

Daisy stopped.

The bells hesitated. There came a tentative *ching*, followed by silence and then another *ching-ching*.

Daisy ran, her yellow hair flying.

The houses disappeared, replaced by a row of stores with jolly front windows and Christmas-treed displays. Lights blinked. Above one store a plastic Santa drawn by plastic reindeer rose, landed, rose, landed.

Ching-ching.

The library budded into view. White-coated brick, its crystal windows were filled with cutouts of Christmas trees and holly.

At the top of the steps, the doorway stood open.

Daisy climbed, entered.

Outside, the ghoul-bells chimed.

Ching-ching.

Ching-ching.

Ching.

She heard the smooth stop of sleigh-skis in the snow.

The library door loomed wide.

Someone stepped into it.

"Daisy?" a voice called coldly. It was a voice she knew.

"Daisy?" it spoke again. Icicles formed in the corners; snow sprinkled down from the ceiling. It was the voice that had spoken to her.

Daisy pushed past the empty librarian's desk, knocked over the silver Christmas tree on the counter. She dove under the tasseled red rope into the children's section. Bright book covers glared at her. Babar the elephant walked a tightrope, the bulb-like faces of Dr. Seuss characters grinned, Huckleberry Finn showed off his inviting raft to his hulking friend Jim. "I wish I could be with them," Daisy thought; but nothing happened.

Behind her, the voice, closer, called again in chilly singsong:

"Daisy, Daisy, it's Christmas always!"

"No!" Daisy hissed to herself fiercely. She crawled under one stack of books that had been left to spill against a bookcase, making an arch. Behind it were more books—Hardy Boys and Nancy Drews, two *Treasure Islands*, one *Robinson Crusoe* tilted at an angle. Behind them a pile of *National Geographic* magazines, with color covers.

Daisy burrowed her way into the magazines, covered herself with books and periodicals, made a fort of the Hardy Boys with a fortress gate made of *The Wind in the Willows*.

Steps clacked closer against the polished oak floor.

"Where are you?" the cold voice sang.

"Christmas all the time!

"Always Christmas!

"Daisy . . ."

The footsteps ceased.

The Hardy Boys were lifted away.

"Daisy . . ."

A hard hand reached down to fall on her. She felt how death-cold he was. His suit was red ice; he wore a red cap at a jaunty angle.

His face was white, his ice-blue eyes were arctic circles filled with swirling frost.

"I wish it was spring! I wish it was April!"

"Christmas always," he said, smiling a sharp blue smile.

"I wish I could kill you!"

With her two small hands Daisy threw *The Wind in the Willows* up at him. A corner of the book hit his cold, smoky eye and he staggered back.

Miraculously, amazingly, he fell. There was a shatter like an icicle hitting the sidewalk. There was the *ching* of a million tiny bells.

He lay silent.

He lay . . . dead.

Daisy got up to see a dying blizzard blowing in his eyes. A cold blue hand lifted momentarily, reached toward her—and fell back, cracking up and down its length.

He dripped melting water.

Daisy breathed.

Outside, a bird sang.

Daisy crawled under the book arch, under the red tassel. She ran past the empty desk, the fallen silver tree, out the yawning door.

The sky was growing blue. A squirrel ran past. A blackbird dipped low, squawked and didn't fall.

It was April.

Spring.

Christmas was leaving the world.

Balsam scent grew sour and stale. The snow grew old-gray and slushy. Winter was old; the house lights, round wreaths, tinsel grew dim and left-out-too-long. In the middle of "Have Yourself a Merry—" the calliope ground to a halt.

At the horizon, the huge red ball was less shiny-bright.

His sleigh stood in front of the library. It was ice-white and red, lined with ice bells, pulled by ice reindeer. It shivered as Daisy climbed into it and snapped the reins.

"Take me to them," she said.

The sleigh shuddered into melting life.

Spring was exploding around her. They went over miles of white earth turning to green. The air was warm as hay. Fish leaped in blue-clear ponds, orange-yellow flowers burst from the ground, leaves generated spontaneously. Daisy wondered if, back in her cellar, watermelons were sprouting everywhere and hoes and shovels were dancing up the stairs to reach the loamy soil.

Beneath Daisy, the ice sleigh dripped into the ground. The soil drank it up—bells, reindeer and all. Daisy leaped from the last puddle of it, new green grass like springs pushing at her feet.

Over a short hill, touching the spring sky—and there was the red ball.

It was a blown-glass Christmas bulb halfway up the sky. Its glossy crimson was tarnishing. Winter rushed out the tiny door at the bottom, howling, eaten alive by spring. Daisy hugged herself as it blew past.

The dying snowstorm engulfed her, pulled her inside.

She sobbed at what was there.

The ball was filled with frozen Christmas. A *Nutcracker* Christmas tree, with a thousand presents underneath, filled the center of the ball. Its branches sagged. Lights were everywhere, winking out. And lining the walls all the way to the top, were frozen people keeping frozen Christmas.

A spidery white stairway wound up and around, and Daisy stepped onto it. There was the snap of melting ice. She looked in at each block, wiping warm tears of water away with her fingers. In one there was a man with a beard she knew who watered his lawn in the summer each Saturday, even if it rained. His beard was frozen now. He knelt before a Christmas tree, fitting it into its stand. There was a boy who delivered newspapers, caught removing a model airplane from its Christmas wrap. A woman was ice in her rocking chair, a mince pie cradled in her pot-holdered hands—the pie looked good enough to eat. A little girl made garlands out of popcorn. A mother and daughter exchanged Christmas cards.

At the end of the winding stair, at the very top, was—

Timothy.

Daisy gasped. Timothy stared out at her like wax. In his hand he held a limp, flat stocking; he bent to tack it to a rich-oiled mantel above a fireplace. A log fire burned snugly in the grate.

The ice shimmered and softened; Timothy moved.

Beside him, there was an empty space.

As Daisy reached out, the ice hardened again.

"Can't . . . unwish . . . ," Timothy said before his mouth froze closed.

Outside, she heard the bells.

Winter came rushing back. The air glinted like clear cold crystal. The tarnished ball grew metal-shiny. On the Christmas tree, limp pine boughs stiffened, grew tall. Nearby, in the walls, in the air, the calliope played "God Rest Ye Merry, Gentlemen."

Ching-ching.

The sleigh moved over the snow with a sound like *wishhhhhhh.*

Ching.

Daisy looked up, and in the red metal glass above her, someone was reflected from far below.

Someone tall and white, with red-ice coat, blue-ice eyes, black-ice boots.

"Ice is water," he explained, in his voice; "water makes ice."

"I wished you were dead!" Daisy screamed.

He put his boot on the stair.

He climbed.

He stood before her.

As he finally put his cold hand on her; as she felt Christmas brighten and stiffen around her; as she felt the red velvet stocking caress her hands, and smelled the wood smoke from the fireplace, and felt Timothy's hand on her arm, telling her not to listen; as ice filled around her and hardened and froze her forever, she heard whispered close by, in a voice she now knew might have been any of a thousand cold or hot voices, a voice that might become any of a thousand cold or hot things, a laughing voice, a voice that was ancient, persistent and patient in its longing for release, "Make a wish."

THE BLIND MAN

by Jessica Amanda Salmonson

The world consisted of loud noises, dangers, and things in the way. Sam's white stick swept the pavement before his every step, but somehow never told him about the dog poo, gum wads, phlegm, or dirty puddles off the ends of curbs. He hadn't been blind long and wasn't very good at it.

First was the garbage can which rattled monstrously when he bumped into it. Then a newspaper vending machine did likewise. Then a metal sign mounted at waist level scraped his hand as he went past. The most common things of life were menacing, deadly.

He hoped he hadn't lost count of the blocks. He heard someone with asthma and asked, "Excuse me. Is this the bus stop?"

No one answered. The person who had been breathing noticeably was suddenly and absolutely still.

"Is this the bus stop?"

In a moment, a man answered sharply, "Yes it is."

"Thank you."

They both stood there in perfect silence. At last a bus came by, snarling, hissing, opening its doors. The silent man didn't move toward it. Sam moved toward the sound of the hissing door and asked, "Is this the Express?"

Mumble mumble.

"Is this the Express?"

The driver shouted, "Yes it is! You getting on?"

Sam got on. He didn't sense other people on the bus. He sat in the first seat in front. The doors hissed shut. The bus jerked away from the curb. Sam rode along for ages, waiting for a certain familiar turn which would signal the halfway point to his destination. He passed the time in thought, but his thoughts weren't pleasant. He remembered the first of two children of the day to comment on his awkward manner of getting around.

"Is that man blind, Mommy?"

"Yes, hon, *shh.*"

"If he's blind, how come he's got glasses? It's not sunny but he's wearing sunglasses!"

"Shh."

He soon removed his dark glasses, self-conscious about them. Not two blocks later he heard some other child say, "You got funny eyes, mister!" Some mother's hand thwacked the boy's face and the sound of bawling faded behind Sam.

Well, he'd made it onto the bus. Everything was such an ordeal. "I'll adjust," he whispered to himself. Within the bus, the world became calmer. The humming of the wheels soothed. Traffic was muted and unthreatening.

It seemed an inordinate length of time and the bus hadn't made one stop. The Express didn't stop often, but there should have been a few transfer points along the way. Nobody was going north, Sam figured. No one but himself.

The sharp bend that marked the halfway point was forever away. Fast as the bus was barreling along, it seemed they should have come upon the curve by now.

Sam said, "We pass Clayton yet?"

"Don't go by Clayton."

Sam's heart sank. "This the number fifteen Express?"

"No, it ain't."

For a long time, Sam didn't say a word.

"What bus is it?"

"Number forty-seven."

"I'm on the wrong bus!"

"Seems like it."

"How do I get to Clayton?"

"Can't get there from here."

"Let me off! I'll catch the bus on the other side of the street!"

"Can't stop. This is the Express."

Sam sat quietly for the longest time, waiting for the bus to come to its first stop. Time passed by and he knew his sister must be worried.

He'd never known a bus to go so far without a single stop. The hum of wheels deadened his sense of time. It seemed that hours had passed. He'd been riding the bus for days.

"How far until we stop?"

No reply.

"How far until we stop, driver?"

The driver didn't answer. Sam grabbed a brace and stood up, pulled himself toward the driver's area, and said, "Sir, I'm blind and afraid of being lost."

No answer.

Sam put a hand forward to tap the driver's shoulder, but couldn't find any shoulder. He took another fumbling step forward and tried to touch the driver again. He only touched a steering wheel. His hand circled the wheel and found no one was driving. He felt the empty seat.

The bus hit a bump which sent Sam staggering backward, plopping down in the front-row seat. He turned his blind eyes toward the back of the bus and called out,

"Is anybody on this bus?"

No one answered.

The Express continued on.

A NIGHT AT THE HEAD OF A GRAVE

by Thomas Sullivan

In his dreams he went inside his body and watched them grow. Cell by cell. On his liver, his bladder, his brain, *his heart* . . . His lungs were studded with them. Some were the size of beads; some looked like flushed cabbages.

He would awaken in a sweat and lie there dehydrated, rust blowing through his veins. After a while he would rise stiffly and dress stiffly and go downstairs stiffly, afraid to touch himself, afraid to eat, afraid to look in the mirror. Finally he would yield to the mirror.

Nothing.

He had never actually been sick. Not a day.

So then he would munch a little toast and drink a little juice to make the pills go down. Vitamins A, C, E. Anti-Cancer Endeavor. But he had never had cancer.

His mother had had it. His father had had it. His great-grandfather, an aunt and two distant cousins had. It had taken him almost a year of letters and research to uncover the cousins. One was a heavy smoker, but the other was like him—a vegetarian, an exerciser, an abstainer from drinks and drugs, a partaker of nostrums. That one had died at the age of thirty-six.

So he had always had an irrational fear of cancer. That was the first thing about Norman Holland. The second thing was that he was very intense.

Intensity was the reason the thing came to him.

That and because of the funeral for his wife. He had always sensed it at funerals: a presence that was not grieved, a gloating malevolence. Things like that waited on the edge of eternity.

He thought about it after his wife's funeral, how he had maybe invited it in even as a boy. He had once healed his dog whom the vet had said would die. His mother thought he had prayed for this, but actually he had made a wish. He had wished that the vet would die instead. The dog lived another six years. The vet died in two months. He was very intense, Norman was. Even then. His mother said that the dog's survival was a miracle, and that his prayers had caused it.

Norman had wished for a lot of things after that, but none of them had ever come to pass. Except that he had gotten the present he had wanted now and then at Christmas and on his birthday and at Easter. And also: frumpy old Mr. Baker, who had successfully sued them over a property line, dropped dead of a heart attack a week after Norman wished him gone.

But then his childhood was over and he had gotten through school, gotten a job, gotten married.

To Lisa Anne.

Who died.

Of cancer.

The dreams—the nightmares—about tumors came back then. And it was at the funeral, two days later, that he sensed a palpable force dodging in and out between the pallbearers' legs and from the edge of the yawning grave—a trickle of dirt rattling down where it touched. But afterward it was still there. After everyone had gone but the diggers waiting impatiently across the road, their shovels not quite hidden behind tombstones, he felt it lingering at the head of the grave.

It was then that he let his intensity out, a rush of fear and hope that fled from him like an escaped inmate flying into the night. Any night. A night at the head of a grave. It thrashed like a confession, blubbering terror and all the pent-up nightmares of aberrant cells accumulating mitotically into a tomb of flesh: *cancer . . . cancer . . . cancer!* And when the rush of feeling was done, he knew that some of the palpable force sitting at the head of the grave had transferred to him, to his hands. And he knew that it was not a freely usable power, but a barely manageable one, like an animal trained by a fragile contortion of its killer instinct to act as guard.

He carried his hands home as if they were separate things then, and laid them by his sides in bed, still not understanding what had happened. Until he dreamed.

The dream told him.

He stood in an immense cancer ward. All about him were the gaunt faces and faucial gasps of the dying. And as if he were the doctor, or some heralded miracle worker, they reached out their cadaverous hands for his touch. He was not afraid of them. On the contrary, the sight of so many beseeching fingers produced a kind of momentum in him, as if he were flying toward them and contact was inevitable. Out went his hands, groping among the bony tubers of a damned and rotting garden. Only, it wasn't damned. Radiance spread like sunshine at his touch. The faucial gasps became wholesome smiles. It was then he noticed the segregation. All the women were on his right, reaching out their right hands; the men on the left, seeking his left. And the radiance spread until in the gathering frenzy he reached across his body with his left hand to take a woman's left. And then his right. Across his body to take a man's right. Too late his cognizance of the sudden silence. The radiance withered and a ghastly gray stained the faces of the two beseechers. Their eyes dulled and sank, their mouths fell open, pain traced tortuous routes along their brows and jaws. Within moments they fell wasted to the ground, already corrupting into the elements. He reached out again, this time right to left, left to right, but each victim he touched quaked and collapsed as though the very moisture of their lives had been boiled dry.

> *Left to left cures a man, kills a woman*
> *Right to right cures a woman, kills a man*

. . . this like a whispered shibboleth told with suppressed glee.

He sat bolt upright in bed. The hands that lay at his sides were possessed! And he stared unseeing into the icy darkness of that region, thinking that he had welcomed an agent of death into his hands. He raised one up to the moonlight. *Or was it life . . . ?*

He had the power to cure cancer.

It was what he had wanted. So, there was a negative side to it. So be it. He was forewarned. Had he subconsciously imposed his own conditions to balance the indebtedness of his soul? Was this the private mechanics of a sense of unworthiness?

He remembered the treachery he had sensed at the edge of eternity that very afternoon, and it seemed to him then that this was the wild card played by a universe whose intricate clockwork began in the chaos of feckless parts. There were always things at large in the universe, random things, catalysts which could undo survival.

"What about me?" he demanded aloud. And spreading both hands against the night, he cried: "How can I cure myself?"

But the full insidiousness of this did not come upon him immediately. It did not come upon him for a day and a night. Because for a day and a night he brooded, and it wasn't until he washed his hands— took the soap in one palm to begin washing—that he realized the full irony.

Left to right . . . right to left. He could give himself cancer as easily as washing his hands.

Or applauding.

Or even praying.

Waves of horror continued to roll over him throughout the next day. His hands were like magnets. They itched to come together. He made fists, he placed them in his pockets, but unless he kept riveted on the danger, some idle task or perverse impulse brought them perilously close again.

At noon he took a pair of tumblers from the cupboard and held each separately while he sat in a chair and cried at the enormity of his simple limitation.

A serrated bread knife lay on the drainboard. *Am I any better off than a man with one hand?* he asked himself and placed the blade against the skin.

The first stroke left a white furrow across the back of his wrist. The second drew blood. The third really began to hurt and he stopped. He was still holding a glass in the hand he had attempted to amputate, and out of anger and frustration he smashed this against the wall. Then he went down to his workbench.

There was a grinder there and a ripsaw. The ripsaw had nearly cost him a finger once when his knuckle grazed it as it was whining down. He could probably sever his wrist in one thrust. Probably. Then he would probably pass out. Probably bleed to death. He opened a can of red enamel and dipped his fingers in, one hand at a time. He let some of the stuff drip off. Then he let the rest dry.

He went upstairs and sat in the living room after that. His hands rested on the chair arms like smoking guns. Twilight came and his fingers no longer looked red. When night fell he would forget and put them together, he thought, or maybe decide he had never received the power at all and willingly slap them together. No. Not willingly. How could he sleep again? A force as diabolical as this would invest his slumbering hands with animation. They would creep like spiders over the sheet and pounce together in a terminal clasp. Dead leaves in an ill wind. He couldn't wait for that. Better to get it over with. But he rose and went to the closet, where, after some moments of searching, he found his winter gloves.

The night was humid, and the gloves were tropical hells. His hands dripped fire in fleece-lined sacks of molten magma. The sheets wound against his flesh like hemp, and hours passed before he was calm enough—exhausted enough—to sleep. If thrashing in a state of unconsciousness can be called sleep. When he awoke, it was with a start and a tingle of raw terror.

Because his hands were no longer in the gloves.

He often slept with them folded over his stomach, but they lay now palms up on either side of him. They were cool and dry. Somehow he knew they had not come together. If they had come together, he would have crumbled into the elements like the victims in his dream. He would writhe with the beginnings of tumors as he had in his nightmares. What alarmed him now was that the gloves had been tight-fitting with snaps at the wrist, and he was stunned that he could have taken them off in his sleep. Or *had* he? He knew then that the night he had sensed at the head of the grave was in the room with him.

He spent the day at home, barely functioning, and when he finally crept up to bed again he taped the gloves on. This time his hands felt like they were in the mouths of lathering dogs. The thrashing to exhaustion before sleep went on as before, but when he surfaced like a diver clawing up from gluey depths, the gloves were still in place. And as he took them off he saw that his fingers were wrinkled and white as if they had been underwater for a long time.

Without thinking, he began rubbing the loose skin off. His palms were so close he could feel the exchange of heat. Suddenly, like a pair of lethal reptiles within killing range, the hands froze. Slowly, with an effort, he pulled them apart. Slowly he drew on the gloves. Slowly he resealed the tape with a tracing finger. So that was how it was going to be, he thought. His right hand literally could not trust his left.

Nothing much changed after that, until he went back to work.

By that time he had begun taping his left hand. Band after band of surgical tape overlapped that palm, and though the skin itched and developed a rash, he felt he had, so to speak, come to grips at last.

But no sooner had he arrived at the little office where he was one of four insurance salesmen than he knew his mistake.

"Norman, Norman," Mr. Kreger, the supervisor, lamented on his behalf, "I'm so sorry about your wife."

And he stuck out his hand.

Without thinking, Norman took it. Right to right with a man. Palm to palm. The very thing that had brought death in his dream. The supervisor mistook the sudden softening of his grip for the weakness of Norman's constitution and clasped the hand all the tighter.

"There, there, Norman," he said, "let us help you. Let your friends help you." Then he saw the tape. "Say, what happened to your other hand?"

"Burned it," Norman mumbled.

That he had just given Mr. Kreger cancer was a certainty. But it wasn't until he was on his way home that it occurred to him he might still cure it. *Left to left cures a man, kills a woman; right to right cures a woman, kills a man.*

The next morning he ripped the tape from his left hand and carefully wound fresh on his right. He hoped, lamely, that Kreger wouldn't remember which had been taped. But . . .

"Now what, Norman? You didn't burn that one as well?"

"Actually . . . yes. I burned that one too."

"Poor Norman. What a lot you've had to suffer. Fate can be cruel. Your left hand seems to have healed nicely, though."

Poor Kreger. What a lot he'll have to suffer, thought Norman. Unless he could cure him. Impulsively he snatched at Kreger's left hand, but somehow he got it palm-side away. He manipulated it in his fingers like a spider wrestling a meal, all of which made Kreger look down in alarm.

"What is it, Norman? What's the matter?"

"I . . . I just want to thank you for being so nice to me yesterday." He almost had it now, but the supervisor tried to pull away. "I mean

. . . what you said about letting my friends help—" He was actually clinging as Kreger wrung his hand in disavowal. "It was just the right thing . . . the right thing to say."

There.

He had it. Palm to palm. Left to left. If it wasn't too late.

But it was.

Kreger saw his doctor the next week. Three months, he was told. The doctor said he had had cancer a long time. He died six weeks later.

So Norman knew he could not cure what he had once caused. Even if he had an extra left hand to cure himself, he could not undo the coming together of his left and right.

And the home office made Norman the new supervisor.

There were better careers for someone with a life-or-death touch. Vocations of love and hate. A political assassin, an avenging religious zealot. Or a healer. Only, in Norman's case, the deciding emotions were fear and guilt.

In mortal terror he quit the post he had earned by causing his predecessor's death. If he had ever believed in a universe governed by discoverable laws, it now crumbled like a thin façade, revealing the feral glee of reckless demigods. He was their pawn, empowered by innocent habit and circumstance to murder. An enormity of guilt loomed over his soul, yet he knew that it wasn't the distant retribution of a roaring hell which made him quail, but the prospect that in some fickle way his demons would cause Norman himself to die of cancer. And it was this that brought him trembling to his knees in search of exculpation.

The name of the hospital was Saint Teresa's.

They had a place of dying there. There was a garden and a fountain. There were benches on all four sides of the fountain and an arcade of columns that encircled the area. All the way around the arcade were the terminal places—windowed rooms with paintings and carpet everywhere but around the beds.

Norman saw his first potential miracle immediately, sitting at the edge of the fountain, as if of all the parched bodies in that place this was the only one to make it to water. The canescent fellow had a haunted look that told Norman he was not yet resigned to die. Sunlight got lost in the soft white fringe on a balding head, and the nearly undressed skeleton made frail ridges in valleys of colorless skin. His cough was almost inaudible.

"Let me help you," Norman said.

The look he got was weary and tinged with anger.

"I'd like to help you," Norman said.

The anger deepened in the man's eyes, but there was searching there too.

"You . . . a doctor?" The words puffed out like the coughs.

"No. I'm a volunteer. They let me in to talk with anyone who's lonely."

Tears glimmered. "You . . . call that . . . help?"

"No. I don't call that help. I can do more than that for you." Norman reached out his left hand, but the withered fingers retracted like claws.

"Don't do that!" the patient croaked with untraceable vigor.

Norman's hand fell on the man's. "Please. I know what I'm doing."

Stoney silence.

Norman dug at the fingers.

"Stop it!" hissed the patient.

"What's wrong with you? I just want to take your hand. It won't hurt. I promise you it won't hurt."

"Stop it!"

Another patient was staring from the arcade. Norman withdrew his hand. The whole thing was absurd. He would be kicked out if he made a fuss.

"You'll probably think I'm crazy," he said then. "You'll probably want me to go, but I really think I can cure you, if you'll just give me your left hand. You see, I have a power, and I can cure—" He broke off because there was genuine horror in the gluey, amber eyes of the patient, horror and a flicker of calculation. "You've got nothing to lose," he insisted.

"How . . . do you know you've got this power?"

There was light in the gluey eyes now.

"Because it was given to me. I wished for it, and it was given to me. You don't have to believe that, but you've still got nothing to lose."

The old man's tongue was emerging like some gray slug, touching the dry lips while his skinny neck craned unsteadily toward Norman. "No," he admitted at last, ". . . nothing to lose."

Slowly he extended his hand.

"Your left one," Norman said. "It has to be your left."

There was a long pause. "You sure?"

"Yes."

Norman's hand accelerated forward like a feather toward an exhaust fan. *Caught!* Palm to palm.

"There," he said, "there."

"I'm cured?"

"Yes."

"I don't feel cured."

"It will probably take a long time for you to convalesce. But I've stopped your cancer." He didn't feel like he'd stopped anything. Actually the touch had left him with a peculiarly unwholesome feeling.

"You're sure it was left to left?"

"Yes, left to left cures a man."

"A *man!*"

Norman thought he heard feral glee in the splashing of the fountain. He saw then that the bone structure before him had once supported a petite face, that the parched lips had been full and beguiling, that the large, gluey eyes were still—

"You're a woman," he flustered. "Dear God, I've given it to you. I've given it to you, and I can't undo it."

She glowered up at him. "You should've asked," she husked. "I'm no worse off than when I did this to myself, but you could've saved me."

He regarded her in total alarm now. "What do you mean you did this to yourself?"

His stomach seemed to be dropping away piece by piece.

"Don't blame me," she whimpered. "You'd have done the same thing."

"What are you saying?"

She turned away.

He stared at her hands in horror then.

"Do you think you're the only one it came to?" she croaked. *"Left to left cures a man, kills a woman . . . only, with me it's the other way around."*

DO I DARE TO EAT A PEACH?

by Chelsea Quinn Yarbro

Weybridge had been burgled: someone—some *thing*—had broken in and ransacked his memories, leaving all that was familiar in chaos. It was almost impossible for him to restore order, and so he was not entirely sure how much had been lost.

Malpass offered him sympathy. "Look, David, we know you went through a lot. We know that you'd like the chance to put it all behind you. We want you to have that, but there are a few more things we have to get cleared up. You understand how it is."

"Yes," Weybridge said vaguely, hoping that, by agreeing, he might learn more. "You have your . . . your . . ."

"Responsibilities," Malpass finished for him. "Truth to tell, there are times I wish I didn't have them." He patted David on the shoulder. "You're being great about this. I'll make sure it's in the report."

Weybridge wanted to ask what report it was, and for whom, but he could not bring himself to say the words. He simply nodded, as he had done so many times before. He opened his mouth, once, twice, then made a wave with one hand.

"We know how it is, old man," Malpass said as he scrutinized Weybridge. "They worked you over, David. We know that. We don't blame you for what you did after that."

Weybridge nodded a few more times, his mind on other things. He eventually stared up at the ceiling. He wanted to tell Malpass and the others that he would rather be left alone, simply turned out and ignored, but that wasn't possible. He had hinted at it once, when they had first started talking to him, and the reaction had been incredulity. So Weybridge resigned himself to the long, unproductive wait.

In the evening, when Malpass was gone, Stone took his place. Stone was younger than Malpass, and lacked that air of sympathy the older man appeared to possess. He would stand by the door, his arms folded, his hair perfectly in place, his jaw shaved to shininess, and he would favor Weybridge with a contemptuous stare. Usually he had a few taunting remarks to make before relapsing into his cold, staring silence. Tonight was no different. "They should have left you where they found you. A man like you—you don't deserve to be saved."

Weybridge sighed. It was useless, he knew from experience, to try to tell Stone that he had no memory of the time he was . . . wherever it was he had been. "Why?" he asked wearily, hoping that some word, some revelation, no matter how disgusting, would give him a sense of what he had done.

"You know why. Treating the dead that way. I saw the photos. Men like you aren't worth the trouble to bring back. They should leave you to rot, after what you did." He shook his head. "We're wasting our time with you. Men like you—"

"I know. We should be left alone." He stared up at the glare of the ceiling light. "I agree."

Stone made a barking sound that should have been a laugh but wasn't. "Oh, no. Don't go pious on me now, Weybridge. You're in for a few more questions before they throw you back in the pond. One of these days you're going to get tired of the lies, and you'll tell us what you were doing, and who made you do it."

Weybridge shook his head slowly. His thin, hospital-issue pajamas made him chilly at night, and he found himself shivering. That reminded him of something from the past, a time when he had been cold, trembling, for days on end. But where it had happened and why eluded him. He leaned back on the pillows and tried to make his mind a blank, but still the fragments, disjointed and terrifying, were with him. He huddled under the covers, burrowing his head into the stacked pillows as if seeking for refuge. He wanted to ask Stone to turn the lights down, but he knew the young man would refuse. There was something about nightmares, and screams, but whether they were his own or someone else's, he was not sure.

"You had any rest since you got here, Weybridge?" Stone taunted him. "I'm surprised that you even bother to try. You have no right to sleep."

"Maybe," Weybridge muttered, dragging the sheet around his shoulders. "Maybe you're wrong, though."

"Fat chance," Stone scoffed, and made a point of looking away from him. "Fat fucking chance."

Weybridge lay back on his bed, his eyes half focused on the acoustical tile of the ceiling. If he squinted, he thought he could discern a pattern other than the simple regularity of perforations. There might be a message in the ceiling. There might be a clue.

Stone stayed on duty, silent for most of his shift, but favoring Weybridge with an occasional sneer. He smoked his long, thin dark cigarettes and dropped the ashes onto the floor. The only time he changed his attitude was when the nurse came in to give Weybridge yet another injection. Then he winked lasciviously and tried to pat her ass as she left the room.

"You shouldn't bother her," Weybridge said, his tongue unwieldy as wet flannel. "She . . . she doesn't want—"

"She doesn't want to have to deal with someone like you," Stone informed him.

Weybridge sighed. "I hope . . ." He stopped, knowing that he had left hope behind, back in the same place his memories were.

Malpass was back soon after Stone left, and he radiated his usual air of sympathy. "We've been going over your early reports, David, and so far, there's nothing . . . irregular about them. Whatever happened must have occurred in the last sixteen months. That's something, isn't it."

"Sure," Weybridge said, waiting for the orderly to bring him his breakfast.

"So we've narrowed down the time. That means we can concentrate on your work in that sixteen-month period, and perhaps get a lead on when you were . . ." He made a gesture of regret and reached out to pat Weybridge on the shoulder.

"When I was turned," Weybridge said harshly. "That's what you're looking for. You want to know how much damage I did before you got me back, don't you?"

"Of course that's a factor," Malpass allowed. "But there are other operatives who might be subjected to the same things that have happened to you. We do know that they were not all pharmacological. There were other aspects involved." He cleared his throat and looked toward the venetian blind that covered the window. It was almost closed, so that very little light from outside penetrated the room.

"That's interesting, I guess," Weybridge said, unable to think of anything else to say.

"It is," Malpass insisted with his unflagging good humor. "You took quite a risk in letting us bring you back. We're pretty sure the other side didn't want you to be . . . recovered."

"Good for me." Weybridge laced his hands behind his head. "And when you find out—*if* you find out—what then? What becomes of me once you dredge up the truth? Or doesn't that matter?"

"Of *course* it matters," Malpass said, his eyes flicking uneasily toward a spot on the wall. "We look after our own, David."

"But I'm not really your own any more, am I?" He did not bother to look at Malpass, so that the other man would not have to work so hard to lie.

"Deep down, we know you are," Malpass hedged. "You're proving it right now, by your cooperation."

"Cooperation?" Weybridge burst out. "Is that what you think this is? I was dragged back here, tranked out of my mind and hustled from place to place in sealed vans like something smuggled through customs. No one asked me if I wanted to be here, or if I wanted you to unravel whatever is left of my mind. Cut the crap, Malpass. You want to get the last of the marrow before you throw the bones out." It was the most Weybridge had said at one time since his return, and it startled Malpass.

"David, I can understand why you're upset, especially considering all you've gone through. But believe me, I'm deeply interested in your welfare. I certainly wouldn't countenance any more abuse where you're concerned." He smiled, showing his very perfect, very expensive teeth. "Anyone who's been through what you've been through—"

"You don't know what it was. Neither do I," Weybridge reminded him.

"—would have every reason to be bitter. I don't blame you for that," Malpass went on as if nothing had been said. "You know that you have been—"

"No, I don't know!" Weybridge turned on him, half-rising in his bed. "I haven't any idea! That's the problem. I have scraps here and there, but nothing certain, and nothing that's entirely real. You call me

David, and that might be my first name, but I don't remember it, and it doesn't sound familiar. For all I know, I'm not home at all, or this might not be my home. For all I know, I never got away from where I was, and this is just another part of the . . . the experiment."

Malpass did not answer at once. He paced the length of the room, then turned and came back toward the head of the bed. "I didn't know you were so troubled," he said finally, his eyes lowered as if in church. "I'll tell your doctors that you need extra care today."

"You mean more drugs," Weybridge sighed. "It might work. Who knows?"

"Listen, David," Malpass said with great sincerity, "we're relying on you in this. We can't get you straight again without your help, and that isn't always easy for you to give, I know."

Weybridge closed his eyes. He had a brief impression of a man in a uniform that he did not recognize, saying something in precisely that same tone of commiseration and concern that Malpass was using now. For some reason, the sound of it made him want to vomit, and his appetite disappeared.

"Is something wrong, David?" Malpass asked, his voice sounding as if he were a very long way off. "David?"

"It's nothing," he muttered, trying to get the other man to go away. "I . . . didn't sleep well."

"The lights?" Malpass guessed, then went on. "We've told you why they're necessary for the time being. Once your memory starts coming back, then you can have the lights off at night. It will be safe then."

"Will it?" Weybridge said. "If you say so."

Malpass assumed a look of long-suffering patience. "You're not being reasonable this morning, David."

"According to your reports, I don't have any reason, period." That much he believed, and wished that he did not. He longed for a sense of his own past, of a childhood and friends and family. What if I am an orphan, or the victim of abuse? he asked himself, and decided that he would rather have such painful memories than none at all.

"What's on your mind, David?" Malpass inquired, still very serious.

"Nothing," he insisted. There were more of the broken images shifting at the back of his mind, most of them senseless, and those that were coherent were terrifying. He had the impression of a man—himself?—kneeling beside a shattered body, pausing to cut off the ears and nose of the corpse. Had he done that? Had he seen someone do that? Had he been told about it? He couldn't be sure, and that was the most frightening thing of all.

"Tell me about it," Malpass offered. "Let me help you, David."

It was all he could do to keep from yelling that his name was not David. But if it was not, what was it? What could he tell them to take the place of David?

"You look terrible. What is it?" Malpass bent over him, his middle-aged features creased with anxiety. "Is there anything you can tell me?"

Weybridge struck out with his arm, narrowly missing Malpass. "Leave me alone!"

"All right. All right." Malpass stepped back, holding up his hands placatingly. "You need rest, David. I'll see that you get it. I'll send someone in to you."

"NO!" Weybridge shouted. He did not want any more drugs. There had been too much in his bloodstream already. He had the impression that there had been a time when his veins had been hooked up to tubes, and through the tubes, all sorts of things had run into his body. He thought that he must have been wounded, or . . . A light truck overturned and burst into flame as a few men crawled away from it. Had he been one of the men? Where had the accident occurred? He put his hands to his head and pressed, as if that might force his mind to squeeze out the things he needed to know.

Malpass had retreated to the door and was signaling someone in the hallway. "Just a little while, David. You hang on," he urged Weybridge. "We'll take care of you."

Weybridge pulled one of his pillows over his face in an attempt to blot out what was left there. Gouts of flame, shouts and cries in the night. Bodies riven with bullets. Where were they? *Who* were they? Why did Weybridge remember them, if he did remember them?

Another nurse, this one older and more massive, came barreling through the door, a steel tray in her hand. "You calm down there," she ordered Weybridge so abruptly that his fear grew sharper.

There was a chill on his arm, and a prick that warmed him, and shortly suffused through him, turning his world from hard-edged to soft, and making his memories—what there were of them—as entrancing as the boardwalk attractions of loop-the-loop and the carousel.

Later that day, when Weybridge babbled himself half awake, they brought him food, and did what they could to coax him to eat it.

"You're very thin, Mr. Weybridge," the head nurse said in a tone that was more appropriate for an eight-year-old than a man in his late thirties.

"I'm hungry," Weybridge protested. "I *am*. But . . ." He stared at the plate and had to swallow hard against the bile at the back of his throat. "I don't know what's the matter."

"Sometimes drugs will do this," the head nurse said, disapproval in her tone and posture.

"You're the ones keeping me on drugs," he reminded her nastily. "You don't know what—"

The head nurse paid no attention to him. She continued to bustle about the room, playing at putting things in order. "Now, we're not to lie in bed all day. Doctor says that we can get up this afternoon for a while, and walk a bit."

"Oh, can *we?*" Weybridge asked with spite. "What else can *we* do?"

"Mr. Weybridge," the head nurse reproached him. "We're simply trying to help you. If you just lie there, then there's very little we can do. You can see that, can't you?"

"What happened to the *we* all of a sudden?" he wanted to argue with her, but lacked the energy. It was so useless that he almost wished he could laugh.

"That's better; you'll improve as long as you keep your sense of humor." She came back to the foot of his bed and patted his foot through the thin blankets. "That's the first step, a sense of humor."

"Sure." How hopeless it seemed, and he could not find out why.

By the time Malpass came back, Weybridge had enough control of himself that he was able to take the man's kind solicitations without becoming angry with him.

"You're going to get better, David," Malpass promised. "We'll be able to debrief you and then you can get away from all this. If you cooperate, we'll make sure you'll have all the protections you'll need."

"Why would I need protections?" And what kind of protections? he added to himself.

Malpass hesitated, plainly weighing his answer. "We don't yet know just how much you did while you were with the other side. There are probably men who would like to eliminate you, men from their side as well as ours. If we put you under our protection, then your chances of survival increase, don't you see that?" He stared toward the window. "It would be easier if we could be certain that you're not . . . programmed for anything, but so far, we can't tell what is real memory and what is . . . random."

"That's a nice word for it: random." Weybridge leaned back against the pillows and tried to appear calm. "Do you have any better idea of what happened?"

"You were in prison for a while, or you believe you were in prison, in a very dark cell, apparently with someone, but there's no way to tell who that person was, or if it's your imagination that there was someone there." He coughed. "And we can't be sure that you were in prison at all."

Weybridge sighed.

"You have to understand, David, that when there are such states as yours, we . . . well, we simply have to . . . to sort out so much that sometimes it—"

"—it's impossible," Weybridge finished for him. "Which means that I could be here for the rest of my life. Doesn't it?"

Malpass shrugged. "It's too early to be thinking about that possibility."

"But it *is* a possibility," Weybridge persisted.

"Well, it's remote, but . . . well." He cleared his throat. "When we have a more complete evaluation, we'll talk about it again."

"And in the meantime?"

"Oh," Malpass said with patently false optimism, "we'll continue to carry on the treatment. Speaking of treatment," he went on, deftly avoiding more questions, "I understand you're going to be allowed to walk today. They want you to work up an appetite, and you need the exercise in any case."

"The head nurse said something about that," Weybridge responded in a dampening way.

"Excellent. *Ex*cellent! We'll tell headquarters that you're improving. That will please the Old Man. You know what he can be like when there's trouble with an operative in the field." He rubbed his hands together and looked at Weybridge expectantly.

"No, I don't know anything about the Old Man. I don't know anything about headquarters. I don't recall being an operative. That's what

I'm being treated for, remember?" He smashed his left arm against the bed for emphasis, but it made very little sound and most of the impact was absorbed by the softness.

"Calm down, calm down, David," Malpass urged, once again speaking as if to an invalid. "I forgot myself, that's all. Don't let it trouble you, please."

"Why not?" Weybridge demanded suspiciously. "Wouldn't it trouble you if you couldn't remember who you were or what you'd done?"

"Of *course* it would," Malpass said, even more soothingly. "And I'd want to get to the bottom of it as soon as possible."

"And you think I don't?" Weybridge asked, his voice rising.

"David, David, you're overreacting. I didn't mean to imply that you aren't doing everything you can to . . . recover. You're exhausted, that's part of it." He reached out to pat Weybridge's shoulder. "I hear you still aren't eating."

The surge of nausea was so sudden that Weybridge bent violently against it. "No," he panted when he felt it was safe to open his mouth.

"The nurses are worried about you. They can give you more IVs, but they all think you'd do better if you . . ." He smiled, making an effort to encourage Weybridge.

"I . . . can't," Weybridge said thickly, trying not to think of food at all.

"Why?" Malpass asked, sharpness in his tone now. "Can't you tell me why?"

Weybridge shook his head, bewildered. "I don't know. I wish I did." *Really?* he asked himself. *Do you really want to know what it is about food that horrifies you so? Or would you rather remain ignorant? That would be better, perhaps.*

"You've got to eat sometime, David," Malpass insisted.

"Not yet," Weybridge said with desperation. "I need time."

"All right," Malpass allowed. "We'll schedule the IV for three more days. But I want you to consent to a few more hours of therapy every day, all right?" He did not wait for an answer. "You have to get to the bottom of this, David. You can't go on this way forever, can you?"

"I suppose not," Weybridge said, fighting an irrational desire to crawl under the bed and huddle there. Where had he done that before? He couldn't remember.

"I'll set it up." Malpass started toward the door. "The Old Man is anxious to find out what happened to you. We have other men who could be in danger."

"I understand," Weybridge said, not entirely certain that he did. What if he was not an agent at all? What if that was a part of his manufactured memories? Or what if he was still in the hands of the other side—what then? The headache that had been lurking at the back of his eyes came around to the front of his head with ferocious intensity.

"We're all watching you, David," Malpass assured him as he let himself out of the white-painted room.

Stone regarded Weybridge with scorn when he heard about the increased therapy sessions. "Taking the easy way, aren't you, you bastard?" He lit a cigarette and glowered at Weybridge.

"It doesn't feel easy to me," Weybridge replied, hoping that he did not sound as cowardly as he feared he did.

"That's a crock of warm piss," Stone declared, folding his arms and directing his gaze at the window. "Anyone does what you did, there's no reason to coddle them."

It was so tempting to beg Stone to tell him what it was he was supposed to have done, but Weybridge could not bring himself to demean himself to that hostile man. "I'm not being coddled."

"According to who?" Stone scoffed, then refused to speak again, blowing smoke toward the ceiling while Weybridge dozed between unrecallable nightmares.

The therapist was a small, olive-skinned gnome named Cleeve. He visited Weybridge just as the head nurse was trying to coax him out of bed to do his required walking. "Out for your constitutional, eh, Mr. Weybridge?" His eyes were dark and glossy, like fur or crushed velvet.

"We're going to walk twice around the nurses' station," the head nurse answered for him. "It's doctor's orders."

Weybridge teetered on his feet, feeling like a kid on stilts for the first time. Dear God, had he ever walked on stilts? He did not know. The effort of a few steps made him light-headed, and he reached out for Cleeve's shoulder to steady himself. "Sorry," he muttered as he tried to get his balance.

"Think nothing of it, Mr. Weybridge," Cleeve told him in a cordial tone. "All part of the service, I give you my word." He peered up at

Weybridge, his features glowing with curiosity. "They've had you on drugs?"

"You know they have," Weybridge said a little wildly. His pulse was starting to hammer in his neck.

Cleeve nodded several times. "It might be as well to take you off some of them. So many drugs can be disorienting, can't they?" He stared at the head nurse. "Who should I speak to about Mr. Weybridge's drugs? I need to know before we start therapy, and perhaps we should arrange a . . . new approach."

The head nurse favored Cleeve with an irritated glance. "You'd have to talk to Mr. Malpass about that."

"Ay, yes, the ubiquitous Mr. Malpass," Cleeve said with relish. "I will do that at once."

Weybridge was concentrating on staying erect as he shuffled first one foot forward, and then the other. His nerves jangled with every move and his feet were as sore as if he were walking on heated gravel. "I don't think I can—"

Both the head nurse and Cleeve turned to Weybridge at once. "Now, don't get discouraged," the head nurse said, smiling triumphantly that she had been able to speak first. "You can take hold of my arm if you think you're going to fall."

Weybridge put all his attention on walking and managed a few more steps; then vertigo overwhelmed him and he collapsed suddenly, mewing as he fell.

"I'll help you up, Mr. Weybridge," Cleeve said, bending down with care. "You appear to be very weak."

"Yes, I suppose I am," Weybridge responded vaguely. He could not rid himself of the conviction that he had to get to cover, that he was too exposed, that there were enemies all around him who would tear him to pieces if he did not find cover. Who were the enemies? What was he remembering?

Cleeve took Weybridge by the elbow and started to lever him into a sitting position, but was stopped by the head nurse. "Now, we don't want to indulge ourselves, do we? It would be better if we stood up on our own."

"That's a little unrealistic," Cleeve protested. "Look at him, woman —he's half starved and spaced out on the chemicals you've been pouring into him."

Hearing this, Weybridge huddled against the wall, arms and knees gathered tightly against his chest. He did not want to think about what had gone into him. The very idea made him cringe. He swallowed hard twice and fanned his hands to cover his eyes.

"They're necessary," the head nurse said brusquely. "Until we know what's happened to this man . . ."

Cleeve shook his head. "You mustn't mistake his condition for the refusal of an enemy. From what I have been told, this man is one of our operatives, yet everyone is behaving as if he were a spy or a traitor." He steadied Weybridge with his arm. "When it's certain that he's been turned, then we can do what must be done, but not yet."

The head nurse folded her arms, all of her good humor and condescension gone. "I have my orders."

"And so do I," Cleeve said mildly. "Mr. Weybridge, I'm going to help you back to bed, and then I want to arrange to have a little interview with you. Do you understand what I'm saying?"

It was an effort to nod, but Weybridge managed it; his head wobbled on the end of his neck. "I want . . . to talk to . . . someone." He coughed and felt himself tremble for the strength it cost him.

"Good. I'll return in an hour or so. Be patient." Cleeve gave a signal to the head nurse. "Get him back into bed and arrange for an IV. I don't think he's going to be able to eat yet."

The head nurse glared at Cleeve. "You'll take responsibility for him, then? I warn you, I won't be left covering for you if you're wrong."

What were they arguing about? Weybridge asked himself as he listened to them wrangle. What was there to be responsible for? What had he done? Why wouldn't anyone tell him what he was supposed to have done? He lifted one listless hand. "Please . . ."

Neither Cleeve nor the head nurse paid him any heed. "You'll have to tell Malpass what you're doing. He might not approve."

Cleeve smiled benignly. "I intend to. As I intend to ask for permission to remove Mr. Weybridge from this wing of the hospital. I think we can do more with him in my ward." He turned toward Weybridge. "Don't worry. We'll sort everything out."

"What . . . ?" Weybridge asked, frowning. He felt very tired, and his body ached in every joint. He supposed he was suffering from malnutrition, but there was more to it than that. Even as the questions rose again, his mind shied away from them. There was so much he could not understand, and no one wished to explain it to him. He pulled himself back onto the bed, pressing his face into the pillow, and nearly gagging on the carrion smell that rose in his nostrils. He retched, gasping for air.

"That's enough of that," the head nurse said with unpleasant satisfaction. "When Mr. Malpass takes me off this case, I'll stop giving him drugs, but for the time being, it's sedation as usual. Or do you want to argue about it, Mr. Cleeve?"

Weybridge was sprawled on the bed, his face clammy and his pulse very rapid. His face was gaunt, his body skeletal. He was like something from deep underwater dragged up into the light of day. "I . . . I . . ."

Cleeve sighed. "I'm not going to oppose you, Nurse. Not yet. Once I talk to Mr. Malpass, however—"

The head nurse tossed her head. "We'll see when that happens. Now you leave this patient to me." She gave her attention to Weybridge. "We're too worn out, aren't we?"

Weybridge hated the way she spoke to him but had not strength enough to protest. He waited for the prick in his arm and the warm bliss that came with it. There was that brief respite, between waking and stupor, when he felt all the unknown burdens lifted from his shoulders. That never lasted long—once again, Weybridge felt himself caught in a morass of anguish he did not comprehend.

The walls were thick, slimy stone, and they stank of urine and rats. His own body was filthy and scabbed, his teeth rattled in his head and his hair was falling out. He shambled through the little space, maddened by fear and boredom. Someone else cowered in the darkness, another prisoner—was he a prisoner?—whose?—why?—or someone sent to torment him. He squinted in an effort to see who it was, but it was not possible to penetrate the shadows. He thrashed on his clean, white bed, believing himself in that dreadful cell—if he had been there at all.

Malpass was standing over Weybridge when he woke with a shout. "Something, David? Are you remembering?"

"I . . ." Weybridge shook his head weakly, trying to recapture the images of his dreams, but they eluded him. "You . . ." He had seen Malpass' face in the dream, or a face that was similar. He had no idea if the memory was valid, or the dream.

"We're having a little meeting about you this morning, David," Malpass said heartily. "We're reviewing your case. The Old Man is coming to hear what we have to say."

Weybridge could think of nothing to say. He moved his head up and down, hoping Malpass would go on.

"Cleeve wants you over in his division. He thinks he can get at the truth faster with those suspension tanks of his and the cold wraps. We'd rather keep you here on drugs, at least until you begin to . . . clarify your thoughts. However, it will be up to the Old Man to decide." He gave Weybridge's shoulder another one of his amiable pats. "We'll keep you posted. Don't worry about that. You concentrate on getting your memory in working order."

There was a fleeting impression of another such promise, from another man—or was it Malpass?—that winked and was gone, leaving Weybridge more disoriented than before. Who was the man he had seen, or thought he had seen? What had he done? Or was it simply more of the confusion that he suffered? "How soon will you know?"

"Soon," Malpass said, smiling. "Today, tomorrow. They're going to put you on IV for a while this morning. This evening, they want you to try eating again."

"I can't," Weybridge said at once. "No food." He was sick with hunger; he could not endure the thought of food. "I can't."

"The head nurse will look after you," Malpass went on, blithe as a kindergarten teacher. "We're going to take Stone off for this evening, and Cleeve will stay with you. He wants a chance to talk to you, to study your reactions."

"Cleeve?" Weybridge repeated.

"He saw you yesterday," Malpass reminded him sympathetically, his face creasing into a mask of good-hearted concern. "You remember speaking with Cleeve, don't you?"

"Yes," Weybridge said, ready to weep with vexation. "I haven't forgotten. It's the other things that are gone."

"Well, possibly," Malpass allowed. "You don't seem to recall coming here. Or have you?"

"I . . ." Had there been an ambulance? A plane? He was pretty sure he had been in a plane, but was it coming here, or had there been a plane earlier, before he had done—whatever it was he had done? Had he flown then? He was certain that he could recall looking down from a great height—that was something. He tried to pursue the image without success.

"Don't work so hard, you only make it more difficult," Malpass admonished him. "You don't need that extra stress right now. If you get frustrated, you won't be able to think clearly about your treatment and getting better."

"I don't think clearly in any case, frustrated or not," Weybridge said with great bitterness.

"We're trying to do something about that, aren't we?" Malpass said, smiling once again. "You're in the best hands, you're getting the finest care. In time, it will come back. You can be sure of that."

"Can I? And what if it doesn't?" Weybridge demanded.

"David, David, you mustn't think this way. You'll straighten it all out, one way or another," Malpass said, moving away from Weybridge. "I'll drop in later, to see how you're doing. Don't let yourself get depressed, if you can help it. We're all pulling for you." With a wave, he was gone, and Weybridge longed for a door he could close, to keep them all out.

There was a new nurse that afternoon, a woman in her mid-thirties, not too attractive but not too plain, who regarded him with curiosity. She took his temperature, blood pressure and pulse, then offered to give him a sponge bath.

"I'll take a shower, later," he lied. He did not like the feeling of water on his skin, though why this should be, he was unable to say. He knew he was a fastidious person and the smell of his unwashed skin was faintly repulsive.

"It might be better if you let me do this for you," she said unflappably. "As long as you're hooked up to that IV, you should really keep your arm out of water. It won't take long. And I can give you a massage afterward." She sounded efficient and impersonal, but Weybridge could not bear the thought of her touching him.

"No, thanks," he said, breathing a little faster. What was making him panic?

"Let me give it a try. Dr. Cleeve suggested that we give it a try. What do you think? Can we do your feet? If that's not too bad, we'll try the legs. That's reasonable, isn't it?"

Both of them knew it was, and so he nodded, feeling sweat on his

body. "Go slow," he warned her, dreading what she would do. "If I
. . ."

She paid no attention to him. "I realize that you're not used to
having a woman bathe you, but after all, your mother did, and this isn't
much different, is it?" She had gone into the bathroom while speaking
and was running water into a large, square, stainless-steel bowl. "I'll
make it warm but not hot. And I'll use the unscented soap. I've got a
real sponge, by the way, and you'll like it. Think about what it can be
like with a big, soft sponge and warm water."

The very mention of it made him queasy, but he swallowed hard
against the sensation. "Fine," he panted.

The nurse continued to get the water ready for him. "You might not
think that you'll like it at first, but you will. I've done work with other
. . . troubled patients and in this case, you're easy to deal with. You
don't make any unreasonable demands or behave badly." She was coming back to him now, carrying the pan of soapy water. "It won't be so
hard. I promise." She flipped back his covers, nodding at his scrawny
legs. "Feet first, okay?"

He did not trust himself to answer her; he gestured his resignation.

"Left foot first. That's like marching, isn't it?" She laughed as she
reached out, taking his ankle in her hand. "The water is warm, just as I
said it would be." She lifted the sponge—it was a real sponge, not one
of the plastic ones—and dribbled the water over his foot.

Weybridge shrieked as if he had been scalded, and jerked away from
her. "No!"

"What's wrong?" she asked, remaining calm.

"I . . . I can't take it. I don't know why, but I can't." He felt his
heart pounding against his ribs as he gasped for air. "I can't," he
repeated.

"It's just water, Mr. Weybridge," the nurse pointed out. "With a
little soap in it."

"I know," he said, trying to sound as reasonable as possible. "But I
can't."

"The way you can't eat, either?" she asked, curious and concerned.
"What is it about water? Or food, for that matter?"

"I wish I knew," he sighed, feeling his heartbeat return to a steady,
barely discerned thumping.

"Can't you figure it out?" She moved the pan of bathwater aside. "Can you tell me anything about it, Mr. Weybridge?"

He shook his head. "I wish I could. I wish I could tell someone what it was. I might be able to get rid of it if I knew what it was." His eyes filled with tears and he turned away from her in shame.

"Why would food and water do this to you?" she mused, not addressing him directly, yet encouraging him.

"There was . . . something that happened. I don't . . . remember, but it's there. I know that it's there." He brought his hands to his face so that he would not have to let her see his expression. He had a quick vision—perhaps not quite a vision, but an image—of a man with a large knife peeling the skin off someone's—his?—foot, grinning at the screams and maddened profanities his victim hurled at him. Weybridge's skin crawled, and after a short time, he pulled his foot out of the nurse's hands. "I can't," he whispered. "I'm sorry. It's not you. I just can't."

"But . . ." she began, then nodded. "All right, Mr. Weybridge. Maybe we can take care of it another time. It would be sensible to tend to this, don't you think?"

"Sure," he said, relieved that he had postponed the ordeal for a little while.

"What's the matter, though? Can you tell me?" Her expression was curious, without the morbid fascination he had seen in the eyes of Malpass and Cleeve.

"I wish I could. I wish I knew what was happening to me. I wish I . . . I wish it was over, all over." He clasped his hands together as if in desperate prayer. "I've tried and tried and tried to figure it out. I have what are probably memories of doing something terrible, something so ghastly that I don't want to think about it, ever. But I don't know what it was, really, or if it ever really happened, or if it did, it happened to me. There are times I'm sure it was someone else and that I've merely . . . eavesdropped on it. And other times, I *know* I did it, whatever it is, and . . . there are only bits and pieces left in my mind, but they're enough." It was strangely comforting to say these things to her. "I've heard that murderers want to confess, most of them. I'm willing to confess anything, just to know for sure what happened, and maybe, why."

The nurse looked at him, not critically but with deep compassion.

"They're speculating on what's real and what isn't: the doctors and the . . . others here. Some of them think you've blocked out your trauma, and others believe that you're the victim of an induced psychosis. What do you think?"

"I don't know what to think. It's driving me crazy, not knowing." He said this quite calmly, and for that reason, if no other, was all the more convincing.

"Do you want to talk about it—I mean, do you want me to stick around for a while and try to sort out what went on when you were—" She stopped herself suddenly and her face flushed.

"Are you under orders?" Weybridge asked. "Are you doing this because they told you to?"

"Partly," she said after a moment. "I shouldn't tell you anything, but . . . they're all using you, and it troubles me. I want to think that you're doing your best to get to the bottom of your . . . your lapses. I don't like the way that Malpass keeps glad-handing you, or the way Cleeve treats you like a lab animal." She had taken hold of the thin cotton spread and now was twisting the fabric, almost unconsciously.

"Are they doing that?" Weybridge asked, not really surprised to learn it.

"They are," she said.

Weybridge nodded slowly, wondering if this kind nurse was just another ploy on Malpass' or Cleeve's part to try to delve into his missing past. He wavered between resentment and hope, and finally said, "Which of you is supposed to be Rasputin and which is supposed to be the saint? That's the usual way, isn't it? One of you convinces the poor slob you're interrogating that you're on his side and the other one is the bad guy, and by pretending to be the guy's friend, you get him to open up." He slammed his fists down onto the bed, secretly horrified at how little strength he had. "Well, I wish I could open up, to any of you. I wish I could say everything, but I can't. Don't you understand that, any of you? I can't. I don't remember." There were only those repugnant, terrifying flashes that came into his mind, never for very long, never with any explanation, but always there, always genuine, and always leaving him so enervated and repelled that he wanted to be sick, and undoubtedly would have been, had he anything left in his stomach to give up. "God, I don't even know for certain that we're all on the same side."

"Of course we are, David," the nurse protested.

"You'd say that, no matter what," Weybridge muttered. "You'd claim to be my friend, you'd make me want to confide in you, and all the time it would be a setup, and you'd be bleeding me dry, getting ready to put me on the dust heap when you're through with me. Or maybe you want to turn me, or maybe I turned, and you're with my old side, trying to find out how much I revealed to the others. Or maybe you think I was turned, and you're trying to find out."

"What makes you think you were active in espionage?" the nurse said to him. "You're talking like someone who has been an operative. Were you?"

"How the hell do I know?" Weybridge shot back. "Everyone here acts as if I was some kind of spy or intelligence agent or something like that. I've been assuming that I was."

"Suppose you weren't?" She stared at him. "Suppose it was something else entirely."

"Like what?" Weybridge demanded.

The door opened and Malpass stepped into the room. "Hello, David. How's it going?"

The nurse gave Malpass a quick, guilty look. "I was trying to give Mr. Weybridge a massage," she said.

"I see," Malpass said with sinister cordiality. "What kind of luck are you having?"

"It seems to bother him, so . . . ." She got off the bed and smoothed the covers over his feet.

"Well." Malpass shook his head. "Tomorrow might be better. There are several things we're going to try to get done this evening, and it would be better if you had a little nap first, David." He motioned to the nurse to leave and watched her until she was out of the room. "Did she bother you, David?"

"She was nice to talk to," Weybridge said in a neutral tone, suddenly anxious to keep the nurse out of trouble. Whatever she was, she was the only person he had met who had been genuinely—or appeared to be genuinely—interested in him as a person.

"That's good to know. It's fine that you're talking to someone," Malpass said, smiling more broadly than before.

"You'll make sure she doesn't get in trouble for talking to me, won't you?"

Malpass' eyebrows rose. "Why, David, what makes you think that she'd be in trouble for a thing like that?"

Weybridge frowned. "I don't know. You're all so . . . secretive, and . . . odd about what you want out of me."

"David, David," Malpass said, shaking his head. "You're letting your imagination run away with you. Why would we want to do such a thing to you? You're sounding like you regard us as your jailers, not your doctors. We want you to improve. No one wants that more than we do. But can't you see—your attitude is making everyone's job more difficult, including your own. You're letting your dreams and fears take over, and that causes all sorts of problems for us. If I could find a way to convince you that you're creating chimeras . . ."

"You'd what?" Weybridge asked when Malpass did not go on.

Malpass made a dismissing gesture. "I'd be delighted, for one thing. We all would be." He cocked his head to the side. "You believe me, don't you?"

Weybridge shrugged. "Should I?"

"Of course you should," Malpass assured him. "God, David, you'd think you were being held in prison, the way you're responding. That's not the case at all. You know it's not."

"Do I?"

"Well, think about it, man," Malpass said expansively. "You're being taken care of as thoroughly as we're able. We want you to get better, to get well and be independent. I think everyone here is pulling for you, and . . . well, David, they are all very concerned for you. Everyone hopes that you'll be over this . . . problem soon." He gave Weybridge his most sincere look. "You're a very special case, and we all want to see you get well, entirely well."

"Un-huh," Weybridge said, looking away from Malpass. "And what will happen to me when I get well? Where will I go?"

"Back home, I would guess," Malpass said, trying to give this assertion an enthusiastic ring.

"Back home," Weybridge echoed. Where was that? What was his home like? "Where do . . . did I live?"

"You mean, you don't remember?" Malpass asked, apparently shocked by this question.

"Not really. I wouldn't be asking if I did," he said testily. "And don't coddle me with your answers. That won't help me at all." He folded his arms, taking care not to press on the IV needle taped just below his elbow.

"Well, you live in a small city about . . . oh, eight hundred miles from here. It's on a river. The countryside is rolling hills. The city has a very large textile industry, and most of the agricultural land in the immediate area is devoted to sheep ranching. There's also a good-sized university. You were an assistant professor there for four years. Do you remember any of this?" Malpass asked. "You're frowning."

Weybridge tried to recall such a place and found nothing in his mind that had anything to do with a small city near a river, or a university. "What did I teach?"

"Physics" was Malpass' swift answer. "Astrophysics. You were lured into the private sector to help develop hardware for space exploration. You were considered to be very good at your work."

"Then, how in hell did I end up here?" Weybridge demanded, his voice shrill with desperation.

"That's what we'd all like to know," Malpass said, doing his best to sound comforting. "Your . . . affliction is a real challenge to us all."

"When did I become an intelligence agent, if I was teaching and then doing space research in industry? What was the name of the university where I taught? What city did I live in? What company did I go to work for? Who was my boss?"

"Whoah there, David," Malpass said, reaching out and placing his thick hand on Weybridge's shoulder. "One thing at a time. First, the Old Man has decided that, for the time being, we're not going to give you too many names. It would be distracting, and you might use the information to create . . . false memories for yourself based on the names instead of your recollections. You can see the sense in that, surely."

"I suppose so," Weybridge said sullenly. "But what the fuck does that leave me?"

"In time, we hope it will restore your memories. We want that to happen, all of us." He gripped a little tighter, giving Weybridge's shoulder a comradely shake, doing his best to buck his charge up. "When you can name your university, the head of your department, then we'll know we're getting somewhere."

"Why did I become an agent? Or did I?" He had not intended to ask this aloud, but the words were out before he could stop them. "Is this some kind of ruse?"

"Of course not," Malpass declared.

"You'd say that whether it was or not," Weybridge sighed. "And there's not any way I can prove the contrary." He lowered his head. "The bodies. Where were they? Whose were they?"

"What bodies, David?" Malpass asked, becoming even more solicitous.

"The ones I see in my dreams. The ones with . . . pieces missing. There are some in cells and some in . . . trenches, I guess. It's . . . not very clear." He felt the sweat on his body, and smelled his fear.

"Can you tell me more about them?" Malpass urged. "What do you remember?"

Hands on the ground, just hands, with palms mutilated; a torso with the striations of ropes still crossing the chest; a child's body, three days dead and bloated; scraps of skin the color of clay sticking to rusty chains; a man on a wet stone floor, his back and buttocks crosshatched with blood-crusted weals; a woman, hideously mutilated and abused, lying on her side, legs pulled up against her chest, waiting for death: the impressions fled as quickly as they came. "Not very much," Weybridge answered, blinking as if to banish what he had seen.

"Tell me," Malpass insisted. "You've got to tell me, David. The Old Man has been asking about your ordeal, and if I can give him something—anything—he might decide to . . ." He did not go on.

"To what?" Weybridge asked. "Or can't you tell me that, either?"

"I . . . haven't been given permission," Malpass said in an under voice. "I'll need to get it if I'm going to explain what it is the Old Man needs to know."

This was the first time Weybridge had ever seen Malpass display an emotion akin to fear, and in spite of himself, he was curious. "Why should the Old Man care what I remember? He has me where he wants me, doesn't he?"

"Well, sure, but we don't want you to have to remain here indefinitely," Malpass said uneasily, attempting to make a recovery. "We're all . . . doing our best for you."

Weybridge shook his head. "That's not enough, Malpass. You're holding back too much. I don't want to say anything more until you're a little more forthcoming with me." It was exciting to defy Malpass, so Weybridge added, "I want the lights out at night. I need sleep."

"I'll see if it can be arranged," Malpass hedged, moving away from the bed, where Weybridge sat. "I'll let you know what we decide."

What had he said? Weybridge wondered. What had caused the change in the affable Mr. Malpass? He could not find the answer, though it was obvious that something he had triggered disturbed the man profoundly. "Is there something you'd like to tell me, Malpass? You seem distraught."

"I'm . . . fine, David. You're probably tired. I'll let you have a little time to yourself, before they bring you your supper."

Was it Weybridge's imagination, or was there a trace of malice in Malpass' tone of voice? He watched Malpass retreat to the door and hover there, his hand on the latch. "What is it?"

"Nothing," Malpass said fervently.

"I'm interested in what it is the Old Man wants to know. Find out if you can tell me. Maybe we can all work together if you're not so secretive with me." He was almost light-headed with satisfaction as he saw the door close behind Malpass.

The afternoon hours dragged by; Weybridge remained in solitude, the IV unit by his bed his only company. He would have liked to have something to read, but this had been refused when he asked the first time, and Weybridge had not renewed his request. He lay back against the skimpy pillows and stared up at the ceiling, trying to make patterns and pictures of the play of light and shadow there.

About sunset, Dr. Cleeve entered the room, his pursed mouth giving him the look of an overstuffed bag with a hole in it. "I see you are alone," he said.

"Is that unusual?" Weybridge asked angrily. "Did you think someone else would be here?"

"Under the circumstances, yes, I did," Dr. Cleeve said with great meaning. "The Old Man isn't satisfied with your progress. He's about ready to give up on you, and so is Malpass."

"Give up on me? How? Why?" In spite of himself, he felt worried by this announcement.

"You're not telling them what they want to know, what they need to know. They think you've been turned and that you're simply playing with them to gain your new masters some time."

"That's not true!" Weybridge protested, trying to get to his feet. "It's not possible! I don't know what I did, I don't know why I'm here, I don't even know who you are, or who I am. What do I have to do to make you believe that?" His pulse throbbed in his head and his eyes ached. There were the images, the memories of so much horror that he could not bear to look at them directly, but that proved it—didn't it?—that he was not deceiving them.

"Mr. Weybridge," Dr. Cleeve soothed. "You're overwrought. I can understand how that would be, but clearly you can see that you are not on very firm ground." He reached over and patted Weybridge's arm, just below the place where the IV needles were taped. "I see that your veins are holding up fairly well. That's something. A man in your condition should be glad that we do not yet have to cut down for a vein."

"It . . ." There was a fleeting vision of arms and legs, tattered remnants of bodies floating on a sluggish current, catching against river reeds, piling up, then drifting on.

"What is it, Mr. Weybridge?" Dr. Cleeve asked intently. "What is happening to you now?"

Weybridge shook his head. "I . . . it's gone now. It's nothing." He felt the sweat on his forehead and his ribs, and he could smell it, hating the odor for its human aliveness.

"Mr. Weybridge," Dr. Cleeve said, folding his arms and regarding Weybridge through his thick glasses, "are you willing to let me try an . . . experiment?"

"How do you mean, 'an experiment'?" Weybridge asked, suspicious in the depths of his desperation.

"There are ways that we can . . . accelerate your mind. We could find out what has truly happened to you, and what you have done. The danger is that if you have been turned, we will know about it, unquestionably, and you will have to face the consequences of your act, but the waiting would certainly be over." He studied Weybridge with increasing interest. "It would not be difficult to do, simply a bit more risky than what we have been doing up till now."

"And what is the risk?" Weybridge asked, wishing he knew more about Dr. Cleeve—any of them—so that he could judge why the man had made this offer.

"Well, if the suppressed memories are traumatic enough, you could become psychotic." He spread his hands wide in mute appeal. "You could still become psychotic just going on the way you are. It may, in fact, be that you are already psychotic. There's really no way of knowing without taking certain risks, and this, at least, would end the suspense, so to speak." He tried to smile in a way that would reassure Weybridge, but the strange, toothy unpursing of his mouth was not reassuring.

"I'll have to think about it," Weybridge hedged.

"Let me suggest that you do it very quickly. The Old Man is anxious to have your case resolved, and his way would most certainly do you permanent damage." Dr. Cleeve watched Weybridge closely. "If you have not already been done permanent damage."

"And we won't know that until we try one of the techniques, right?" Weybridge ventured, his tone so cynical that even he was startled by the sound of it.

"It is the one sure way." Dr. Cleeve paused a moment. "It may not be that you have any choice."

"And it is really out of my hands in any case, isn't it?" He sighed. "If I say yes to you, or if I wait until the others, the Old Man—whoever he is—makes up his mind to put my brain through the chemical wringer. Which might have been done already. Did you ever think of that?"

"Oh, most certainly we've thought of it. It seems very likely that there has been some . . . tampering. We've said that from the first, as you recall." He smacked his fleshy palms together. "Well. I'll let you have a little time to yourself. But try to reach a decision soon, Mr. Weybridge. The Old Man is impatient, as you may remember."

"I don't know who the Old Man is. He's just a name people keep using around here," Weybridge said, too resigned to object to what Dr. Cleeve said to him.

"You claim that's the case. That's how the Old Man sees it. He thinks that you're buying time, as I said. He thinks that this is all a very clever ploy and that you're doing everything you can to keep us from following up on your case." He shrugged. "I don't know what the truth of the matter is, but I want to find it out. Don't you?" This last was a careful inquiry, the most genuine question the man had asked since he'd come into the room.

"You won't believe it, but I do," Weybridge said, feeling himself grow tired simply with speaking. He had reiterated the same thing so often that it was no longer making much sense to him. "I have to know what really happened to me, and who I am."

"Yes; I can see that," Dr. Cleeve said with an emotion that approached enthusiasm. "You think about it tonight. This isn't the kind of thing to rush into, no matter how urgent it may appear."

As Weybridge leaned back against the pillows, he was feeling slightly faint, and he answered less cautiously than he might have under other circumstances. "If it gets us answers, do whatever you have to do."

"Oh, we will, Mr. Weybridge," Dr. Cleeve assured him as the door closed on him.

There were dreams and fragments of dreams that hounded Weybridge through the night. He was left with eyes that felt as if sand had been rubbed into the lids and a taste in his mouth that drove what little appetite he possessed away from him, replacing it with repugnance.

Malpass did not come to visit him until midday, and when he arrived, he looked uncharacteristically harried. "You're having quite a time of it with us, aren't you, David?" he asked without his usual friendly preamble.

"I've done easier things, I think." He tried to smile at the other man, but could not force his face to cooperate. "I wish you'd tell me what's going on around here."

"The Old Man wants to take you off the IV unit and see if a few days on no rations will bring you around. I've asked him to give me a few more days with you, but I don't know if he's going to allow it. Three of our operatives were killed yesterday, and he's convinced you can tell him how their covers were blown."

"It wasn't me," Weybridge said firmly, and even as he spoke, he wondered if some of those drastic images stored in his mind where the memories had been might be associated with the loss of the other operatives.

"The Old Man doesn't believe that. He thinks you're still following orders." Malpass licked his lips furtively, then forced them into a half smile that reflected goodwill. "You've got to understand, David. The Old Man simply doesn't buy your story. We've all tried to convince him that you're probably nothing more than a pawn, someone who's been set up to distract us, but that isn't making any headway with the Old Man. He's pissed about the other operatives, you see, and he wants someone's head on the block. If it isn't yours, it may have to be mine, and frankly, I'd rather it was yours." This admission came out in a hurry, as if he hoped that in saying it quickly, he would disguise its meaning.

"And you want this over with, don't you, Malpass?" Weybridge asked, feeling much more tired than he thought it was possible to be. "I want it over with too."

"Then, you'll agree? You'll let them question you again, with drugs so we're sure you're telling us the truth?" He sounded as eager as a schoolboy asking for a day without classes.

"Probably," he said. "I have to think it over. You're going to have to muck about in my mind, and that's happened once already. I don't want to be one of those miserable vegetables that you water from time to time."

Malpass laughed as if he thought this caution was very witty. "I don't blame you for thinking it over, David. You're the kind who has to be sure, and that's good, that's good. We'll all be easier in our minds when the questions have been answered."

"Will we? That's assuming you find out what you want to know, and that it's still worth your while to keep me alive. There are times I wonder if you're on my side or the other side—whoever my side and the other side may be—and if anything you're telling me is true. If you were on the other side, what better way to get me to spill my guts to you than to convince me that you're on my side and that you're afraid I've been turned. You say you're testing me, but it might not be true."

"David, you're paranoid," Malpass said sternly. "You're letting your fears run away with you. Why would we go through something this elaborate if we weren't on your side? What would be the purpose?"

"Maybe you want to turn me, and this is as good a way as any to do it. Maybe I've got information you haven't been able to get out of me yet. Maybe you're going to program me to work for you, and you started out with privation and torture, and now that I'm all disoriented, you're going to put on the finishing touches with a good scramble of my brain." He sighed. "Or maybe all that has already happened and you're going to see what I wrecked for you. And then what? You might decide that it's too risky to let it be known that you've found out what happened, and so you'll decide to lock me up or turn me into some kind of zombie or just let me die."

"You're getting morbid," Malpass blustered, no longer looking at Weybridge. "I'm going to have to warn the Old Man that you've been brooding."

"Wouldn't you brood, in my position?" Weybridge countered, his face desolate.

"Well, anyone would," Malpass said, reverting to his role as chief sympathizer. "Have you been able to have a meal yet?"

The familiar cold filled him. "No," Weybridge said softly. "I . . . can't."

"That'll be one of the things we'll work on, then," Malpass promised. "There's got to be some reason for it, don't you think? David, you're not going to believe this, but I truly hope that you come through this perfectly."

"No more than I do," Weybridge said without mirth. "I'm tired of all the doubts and the secrecy." And the terrible visions of broken and abused bodies, of the panic that gripped him without warning and without reason, of the dread he felt when shown a plate of food.

"Excellent," Malpass said, rubbing his hands together once, as if warming them. "We'll get ready, so when you make up your mind we can get started."

"You're convinced that I'll consent. Or will you do it no matter what I decide?" Weybridge said recklessly, and saw the flicker in Malpass' eyes. "You're going to do it no matter what, aren't you?"

"I'll talk to you in the morning, David," Malpass said, beating a hasty retreat.

There were dreams that night, hideous, incomplete things with incomprehensible images of the most malicious carnage. Weybridge tossed in his bed, and willed himself awake twice, only to hear the insidious whispers buzz around him more fiercely. His eyes ached and his throat was dry.

Dr. Cleeve was the first to visit him in the morning. He sidled up to Weybridge's bed and poked at him. "Well? Do you think you will be able to help me?"

"If you can help me," Weybridge answered, too exhausted to do much more than nod.

"What about Malpass? Are you going to put him off, or are you going to convince him that my way is the right one?" The tip of his nose moved when he spoke; Weybridge had never noticed that before.

"I . . . I'll have to talk to him." He moved his arms gingerly, taking care to test himself. "I want to do what's best."

"Of course you do," Dr. Cleeve declared. "And we've already discussed that, haven't we?" His eyes gloated, though the tone of his voice remained the same. "You and I will be able to persuade the rest of them. Then you'll be rid of your troubles and you can go about your life again instead of remaining here."

"Will I?" Weybridge had not meant to ask this aloud, but once the words were out, he felt relieved. "Or am I speeding up the end?"

"We won't know that until we know what's been done to you, Mr. Weybridge," said Dr. Cleeve. "I'll have a little talk with Malpass and we'll arrange matters."

"When?" Weybridge asked, dreading the answer.

"Tomorrow morning, I should think," he replied, hitching his shoulders to show his doubt.

"And then?" Weybridge continued.

"We don't know yet, Mr. Weybridge. It will depend on how much you have been . . . interfered with." He was not like Malpass, not inclined to lessen the blow. "If there is extensive damage, it will be difficult to repair it. It's one of the risks you take in techniques like this."

Weybridge nodded, swallowing hard.

"Malpass will doubtless have a few things to say to you about the tests. Keep in mind that he is not a medical expert and his first loyalty is to the Old Man."

"Where is your first loyalty?" Weybridge could not help asking.

"Why, to the country, of course. I am not a political man." He cleared his throat. "I hope you won't repeat this to Malpass; he is suspicious of me as it is."

"Why is that?"

"There are many reasons, most of them personal," Dr. Cleeve said smoothly. "We can discuss them later, if you like, when you're more . . . yourself."

Weybridge closed his eyes. "Shit."

"I have a great deal to do, Mr. Weybridge. Is there anything else you would like to know?" Dr. Cleeve was plainly impatient to be gone.

"One thing: how long have I been here?"

"Oh, five or six weeks, I suppose. I wasn't brought in at first. Only when they realized that they needed my sort of help. . . . That was sixteen days ago, when you had recovered from the worst of your wounds but still could not or would not eat." He waited. "Is that all, Mr. Weybridge?"

"Sure," he sighed.

"Then, we'll make the arrangements," Dr. Cleeve said, closing the door before Weybridge could think of another question.

He was wakened that night—out of a fearful dream that he would not let himself examine too closely—by the nurse who had been kind enough to be interested in him and had tried to rub his feet. He stared at her, trying to make out her features through the last images of the dream, so that at first he had the impression that she had been attacked, her mouth and nostrils torn and her eyes blackened.

"Mr. Weybridge," the nurse whispered again, with greater urgency.

"What is it?" he asked, whispering too, and wondering how much the concealed devices in the room could hear.

"They told me . . . they're planning to try to probe your memory. Did you know that?" The worry in her face was clear to him now that he saw her without the other image superimposed on her face.

"Yes, that's what they've— we've decided."

"You agreed?" She was incredulous.

"What else can I do?" He felt, even as he asked, that he had erred in giving his permission. "Why?"

"They didn't tell you, did they? about the aftereffects of the drugs, did they? Do you know that you can lose your memory entirely?"

"I've already lost most of it," Weybridge said, trying to make light of her objections.

"It can turn you into a vegetable, something that lies in a bed with machines to make the body work, a thing they bury when it begins to smell bad." She obviously intended to shock him with this statement, and in a way she succeeded.

"You don't know anything about that," Weybridge said heatedly. "You haven't seen bodies lying unburied in an open grave in a field where the humidity makes everything ripe, including the bodies." He coughed, trying to think where that memory came from. "You haven't been locked in a stone-walled room with five other people, no latrine and not enough food to go around."

"Is that what happened to you?" she asked, aghast at what she heard.

"Yes," he said, with less certainty.

"Did it?"

"I think so. I remember it, pieces of it, anyway." He rubbed his face, feeling his beard scratch against the palms of his hands. Under his fingers, his features were gaunt.

"They'll force you to remember it all, if it happened," she warned him. "Don't you understand? They'll throw you away like used tissue paper when they're done. They don't care what happens to you after they find out what you know. Truly, they won't bother to see you're cared for." She reached out and took him by the shoulders. "If you want to stay in one piece, you've got to get away from here before they go to work on you. Otherwise you'll be . . . nothing when they're through with you, and no one will care."

"Does anyone care now?" he wondered aloud. "I don't know of anyone."

"Your family, your friends, someone must be worried about you. This place is bad enough without thinking that . . ." Her voice trailed off.

"And where is this place? If I got out, where would I be? Don't you see, I have no idea of who these people are, really, or where we are or what it's like outside. No one has told me and I don't remember. Even if I got out, I would have no place to go, and no one to stay with and nothing to offer." His despair returned tenfold as he said these things.

"I'll find someone to take care of you until you remember," she promised him, her eyes fierce with intent.

"And feed me?" he asked ironically. "Do you have a friend with an IV unit?"

"Once you're out of here—" she began.

"Once I'm out of here, I'll be at the mercy of . . . everything. Where are we? Where would I have to go for the Old Man—whoever he is—not to find me and bring me back? It might be worse out there." He shivered. "I don't think I can manage. If I could get out, I don't think I'd be able to get very far before they brought me back."

"We're near a river. We're about fifteen miles from the capital, and—"

"What capital is that?" Weybridge inquired politely. "I don't know which capital you mean."

"*Our* capital, of course," she insisted. "You can get that far, can't you? There are names I could give you, people who would hide you for a while, until you make up your mind what you want to do about . . . everything."

"I don't know about the capital," Weybridge repeated.

"You *lived* there, for heaven's sake. Your records show that you lived there for ten years. You remember that much, don't you?" She was becoming irritated with him. "Don't you have any memory of that time at all?"

"I . . . don't think so." He looked at her strangely. "And for all I know, my records are false. I might not have been here ever, and it could be that I haven't done any of the things I think I have."

"Well, letting them fill you up with chemicals isn't going to help you find out. You'll just get used up." She took his hand and pulled on it with force. "Mr. Weybridge, I can't wait forever for you to make up your mind. If they found out I came in to see you and tried to get you to leave, I'd be in a lot of trouble. You understand that, don't you?"

"I can see that it might be possible." He tugged his hand, but she would not release it. "Nurse, I don't want to go away from here, not yet, not until I can get some idea of who I am and what I did. Not until I can *eat.*"

"But you will be able to if you leave. You're being manipulated, Mr. Weybridge. David. They're doing things to you so that you can't eat, so you'll have to stay here. If only you'd get away from here, you'd find out fast enough that you're all right. You'd be able to remember what really happened and know what was . . . programmed into you. They don't care what comes of their little experiments, and they're not going to give a damn if you go catatonic or starve to death or anything else. That's the way they've been treating agents that they have questions about." She paused. "I have to leave pretty soon. It's too risky for me to remain here. They'll catch me and then they'll . . ." She turned away, her eyes moving nervously toward the door.

Weybridge closed his eyes, but the dreadful images did not fade. There were three naked figures, two of them women, twitching on a stone floor. They were all fouled with blood and vomit and excrement, and the movements and sounds they made were no longer entirely human. "I've been thinking," he said remotely, his throat sour and dry, "that I've been going on the assumption that all the pieces of things I remember, all the horrors, were done to me. But I can't find more than three scars on my body, and if it had happened, I'd be crosshatched and maimed. I've thought that perhaps I *did* those things to others, that I was the one causing the horror, not its victim. Do you think that's possible? Do you think I finally had enough and wouldn't let myself do anything more?" This time when he pulled on his hand, she let him go.

"I can't stay, Weybridge. If you haven't got sense enough to come with me, there's nothing I can do to change your mind. You want to let them do this to you, I can't stop you." She got off his bed, her eyes distraught though she was able to maintain an unruffled expression. "After today, you won't have the chance to change your mind. Remember that."

"Along with everything else." He looked at her steadily. "If you get into trouble because of me, I want you to know that I'm sorry. If I'm right, I've already caused enough grief. I don't know if it's necessary or possible for you to forgive me, but I hope you will."

The nurse edged toward the door, but she made one last try. "They might have given you false memories. They're doing a lot of experiments that way. Or you could be someone else, an agent from the other side, and they're trying to get information out of you before they send you back with a mind like pudding." She folded her arms, her hands straining on her elbows. "You'd be giving in to them for no reason. Hostages, after a while, try to believe that their captors have a good reason to be holding them. That could be what you're feeling right now."

"Nurse, I appreciate everything. I do." He sighed. "But whether you're right or not, it doesn't change anything, does it? I can't manage away from this . . . hospital. I'd be worse than a baby, and anyone who helped me would be putting themselves in danger for nothing. And if you're trying to get me back to the other side, who's to say that I'm one of theirs? Perhaps they want me to do more than has already been done."

She opened the door a crack and peered out into the hall. "I've got to leave, Weybridge."

"I know," he said, filled with great tranquillity. "Be careful."

"You, too," she answered. And then she was gone.

Weybridge lay back against the pillows, his emaciated features composed and peaceful as he waited for the needles and the chemicals and oblivion.

CHARLES L. GRANT is one of the most respected writers and editors in the fields of horror and fantasy. He is the winner of two Nebula Awards for science-fiction writing, a World Fantasy Award as the editor of the original Shadows anthology, and at the most recent World Fantasy Awards he emerged as the winner in the categories of Best Novella and Best Collection (for *Nightmare Seasons,* a collection of his own horror fiction). His most recent novel is *The Tea Party.* In addition to the popular Shadows series, he is also the editor of the anthologies *Terrors* and *Nightmares.* He lives in New Jersey.